# MY BROTHER'S ENVY

## J. L. ROSE

**Good2Go Publishing**

**My Brother's Envy**
Written by J. L. Rose
Cover Design: Davida Baldwin
Typesetter: Mychea
ISBN: 9781943686391
Copyright ©2017 Good2Go Publishing
Published 2017 by Good2Go Publishing
7311 W. Glass Lane • Laveen, AZ 85339
www.good2gopublishing.com
https://twitter.com/good2gobooks
G2G@good2gopublishing.com
www.facebook.com/good2gopublishing
www.instagram.com/good2gopublishing

# DEDICATION

I want to dedicate this book to two guys who really helped me out with this book. First, my roommate and good friend as well as a main character in this book, De'Neair Stanley. I can't forget about you! And also to Erick Collins. I got you, playboy!

## ACKNOWLEDGEMENTS

We did it again, y'all! I first gotta thank my Heavenly Father as always. I want to thank my mentor and friend, Ray Brown. Thanks for everything! I also want to thank my family for everything you all have been doing to hold me down. I love each one of y'all, even those I don't talk to. And to the loyal fans, I thank you with everything that's in me, because without you all, who would J. L. Rose be? Enjoy this book!

Peace!

# MY BROTHER'S ENVY

# PROLOGUE

*Two Weeks Before*

**BRENDA HUNG UP THE** phone after calling her son and receiving his voice message again for the fifth or sixth time. She stood outside on the front porch of her and her husband's house. She could still hear her husband inside going off about the drugs and gun that he found inside her son's bedroom a few hours ago.

Brenda started to call her son's cell phone once more, when she saw the SUV slowly making its way to the front of her house and stopping. She stood staring at the Cadillac SRX but then began shaking her head once the light inside of the SUV went on and she was able to see her nineteen-year-old son and a familiar older woman she knew instantly. Brenda watched her son kiss the older woman, who was the wife of a judge. She folded her arms across her chest as the Cadillac drove off and her son entered the front yard and began making his way up the walk and onto the porch.

"Mom, I know you're—!"

"ReSean, I don't wanna hear your excuses!" Brenda told her son, cutting him off just as the front door opened behind her.

"Brenda, you still ain't—!" James started, but paused after stepping out on the porch, seeing his stepson, and instantly feeling his anger rise. "Boy, you gotta be either real stupid or you really wanna see what the inside of a prison looks like!"

Boss stared at his mother's husband with a blank look. He then shook his head and turned back to his mother, when James grabbed onto his arm and jerked him back around.

"You son of a bitch!" James started, but never got the chance to finish. He never saw the left that his stepson swung, but he certainly felt the pain that exploded in his right eye socket.

"ReSean!" Brenda screamed, seeing her son grab James by the throat with his left hand, only to pull out a chrome gun with his right and shove it into James's cheek.

She rushed to her husband's side and began trying to peel her son's hand free from James's throat.

"ReSean, please! Let him go! You're going to kill him, ReSean!"

Boss heard his mother begging for her husband's life. He shifted his eyes to her, and after seeing the pleading look on her face, he released James's throat and stepped back, when he heard the gasping sound as his mother's husband tried to catch his breath.

Boss then shook his head as he stepped away from both his mother and her husband. He slid his hammer back into the front of his jeans and then snatched up his fitted cap from the floor. James began yelling out threats of calling the police and reporting about the drugs and the gun that he found inside of his bedroom.

"ReSean!" Brenda cried in fear, seeing the look on her son's face.

She left her husband and met her son on his way back over to her husband.

"ReSean, please! Let me handle this!"

Brenda pushed her son from the porch and away from James to the sidewalk. She begged and pleaded with her son to just leave and go to a friend's house until she had time to deal with James. She promised to call him later. Brenda sighed after her son kissed her cheek and turned away walking off. She stood watching him a few moments, but then looked back up at her husband on the porch and saw him on the cordless home phone.

# ONE

**VANITY LOOKED BEHIND HER** only to once again see the handsome milk-chocolate-complexioned guy sitting across the aisle and one seat back from where she sat on the Greyhound bus. She smiled and met his eyes, but she looked away, not wanting to come off like some thirsty female. She stared out her window only to find herself picturing Mr. Handsome's face.

"Can I sit down?"

Vanity swung her head around after hearing the smooth and nice deep voice, only to freeze as she sat staring up into the eyes of the same gorgeous guy who was just sitting across from and behind her. She got control of herself and spoke up. "Um, yeah! You can sit down."

She watched Mr. Handsome as he sat down beside her. He then set his duffel bag on the seat across from them and put his black leather backpack on the floor between his legs. Vanity met his hazel-green-colored eyes after he tipped up his fitted Yankees cap.

"What's ya name, gorgeous?" he asked, showing a smirk-like smile at how shorty was staring at him.

"Vanity," she answered. "What's yours?"

"Boss," he replied.

"Boss!" she asked, giving him a look. "That's your name?"

"My name's ReSean, but I go by Boss," he explained. "You say ya name is Vanity. Does the name go with the actual meaning of the word vanity, or doesn't it?"

"You can relax, ReSean!" Vanity told him, rolling her eyes

playfully and smiling at him. "It's just the name my mother gave me. But answer something. Why do you call yourself Boss?"

"I guess that's just something you have to see for yourself about me in time," Boss told her before asking, "You interested in getting to know me and seeing me again, Ms. Vanity?"

"Getting to know you how, ReSean?" she asked, smiling over at him.

"What do you have in mind, gorgeous?" Boss asked, smiling at Vanity, causing her to look away yet smile harder.

Vanity shook her head, looked back at Boss still smiling, and noticed his deep dimples. "ReSean, I'll be honest with you. I'm talking to somebody right now, but it's nothing serious between us though; so if you're still interested in getting to know me, I would like to see you again," she admitted.

"If that's how I'll be able to see more of you, then I'll take it!" Boss told her, causing Vanity to blush and look away shyly.

* * *

Boss kicked it with the shorty who introduced herself to him as Vanity as they laughed and talked for the rest of the trip. He found out that she was older than him at twenty-three and lived alone. She had a younger sister who lived with their mother and father. Boss was so into vibing with Vanity that it took him a moment to realize the Greyhound bus was pulling into the station.

"We're here already!" Vanity said, also noticing they were pulling inside the Greyhound station.

"You sound disappointed!" Boss said as he stood up from his seat, grabbed his backpack off the floor, and shifted his eyes to look back at Vanity. "How about giving me ya number so we can talk or maybe hook up later?"

"You better call me, too!" Vanity told him, reaching for her purse and pulling out something to write on and with.

Boss grabbed his duffel bag from the seat across from him and Vanity. When he turned back, he saw Vanity standing up and holding out a piece of paper on which she wrote her number. He couldn't help but shift his eyes over her thick, curvy, and yet still toned five foot four and 148-pound body that was a sexy-as-hell 34D-25-42 frame.

"Umm, hello!" Vanity said with a smile, as Boss's eyes were locked directly on her D-cup breasts.

"Yeah!" Boss answered, shifting his eyes from Vanity's perfectly round and perky titties and grabbing the paper from her outstretched hand. "I'll call tonight!"

"You better!" Vanity replied, rolling her eyes playfully at Boss as she reached up inside the overhead compartment to grab her bag, only to feel and smell Boss step up behind her and reach up and grab her Louis Vuitton bag for her.

"Come on!" Boss told her, nodding for Vanity to follow him to the front and catching the smile she gave him as she began following behind him.

Once they arrived at the front door and after the bus driver parked and allowed the passengers to disembark, Boss led Vanity off the bus and onto the crowded platform.

She gently grabbed his arm and asked, "You never told me who you were meeting here? Are you expecting someone?"

"I'm supposed to meet my—"

"Vanity!" Boss and Vanity heard as they both turned around behind Boss to see a tall, mocha-complexioned, bald-shaven man with a sharp goatee walking toward them.

"Malcolm!" Vanity cried in surprise, cutting her eyes to Boss as Malcolm walked up to her and kissed her directly on the lips in front of Boss.

"Damn!" Malcolm said, smiling down at Vanity. "I was wondering if I had to drive up to Atlanta to come get you."

"What are you doing here?" Vanity asked as she slowly pulled away from Malcolm. "I thought Tia was coming to pick me up."

"I told her I wanted to come get you," he told her. "You ready to go?"

"Yeah!" Vanity answered, before turning around and seeing Boss give her a little smile.

Boss held out her bag and said, "I'll call you later, shorty."

Vanity took her bag and watched as Boss walked off with such ease and smoothness.

She was so caught up watching him, until Malcolm interrupted and asked, "So, who's the dude?"

Malcolm glanced back in the direction where Boss went. After no longer seeing him, Malcolm looked back at Vanity, only to have her grab his arm and pull him off heading toward the street.

\* \* \*

Boss watched as Vanity and the guy she called Malcolm left the platform and walked across the street to the parking lot. He shook his head and smirked as he turned and walked into the Greyhound station to look for his supposed father, who he really didn't know but met once before when he was five years old. But according to his mother, his father knew exactly how he looked from pictures she sent him over the years.

Once he got inside the bus station, Boss looked around and expected someone to call out his name. He noticed a bank of pay phones and remembered the piece of paper that his mother gave him with his father's contact number written on it. He headed over to the phones and walked up to an open one. After setting both bags on the ground, Boss dug out the paper and some change to make a call to his father. He picked up the handset, dropped a few coins into the phone, and then dialed the number.

Boss listened to the number ringing once and then twice before the line was answered. Boss froze in both surprise and confusion when he heard a Spanish-speaking woman on the other end of the line.

"Ummm, do you only speak Spanish? Can you speak English?"

Boss heard only Spanish in return from the woman, so he hung up the phone and thought he must have dialed the wrong number. He tried calling the number again, but the phone was answered by the same woman speaking Spanish again.

"What the fuck was that?" Boss said out loud to himself, staring down at the phone a few moments before he dug out some more change, picked up the handset again, and called his mother's cell phone number.

"What the hell?" Boss cried out, hearing that his mother's cell phone was no longer in service.

He tried the number again and received the same message that the wireless customer's phone was no longer in service.

Boss tried his old house number, but he slammed the receiver back down after hearing that the number was disconnected. He stood there a few moments understanding that he wasn't just lied to, but his own mother played him for a complete fool. With reality clear in his mind, he snatched up his bags and headed for the exit.

"What the?" Boss heard someone yell, ignoring a man even after almost hitting him when he shoved open the door.

Boss walked over to the edge of the platform just in time to see a yellow taxi cab driver pass. He whistled and got the cab driver's attention, causing the car to come to a stop in front of him. Boss walked toward the cab as the driver looked out his window.

"Where to buddy?" the cab driver asked his new passenger.

"Take me to a cheap hotel somewhere," Boss told the driver.

He then turned his head and looked out the window as his mind drifted instantly back to the reality of what had been done to him by his own mother.

# TWO

**BOSS FELT THE CHANGE** in the speed of the taxi while walking out of his half-asleep state. He lifted his head and looked out the backseat window, just as the driver was turning into an old-looking motel that was surprisingly crowded with cars and people walking around the parking lot.

"Here we go, buddy!" the cab driver announced, turning in his seat to look back at his passenger.

Boss stared out the window a moment at the hotel and sighed loudly as he shifted his gaze to the meter to see how much he owed. He pulled out a nice-sized bankroll, which was actually all the cash he had with him, and paid the driver his fare.

Boss grabbed his bags and climbed out of the taxi. After he shut the door, he watched the cab pull off and adjusted his fitted cap as he started across the parking lot and headed toward the entrance of the motel. He entered the lobby and saw a small group gathered inside. He ignored the stares from both females and males as well as the flirtatious calls from the females he passed on his way to the front desk.

"Excuse me?" Boss called out to the heavy-set white man who sat behind the front desk watching a small black-and-white television while spitting tobacco juice into a paper cup.

"What can I do for ya, man?" the white man asked with a mouthful of chewing tobacco, never taking his eyes off the little TV.

Boss explained that he needed a room for at least two weeks and that he preferred a room that was in the front of the motel facing the street. Boss paid the cost of the room and then accepted the room key before he turned and left the motel lobby.

Once Boss stepped outside and looked for his new residence, he stopped in front of room number 6 at the end of the hall. He was sliding the key into the lock when he heard a voice.

"Hey, handsome! You want some company?"

He looked over his shoulder and saw a light-skinned woman and a white girl standing in the stairwell staring him down. Boss simply shook his head as he focused back on his room door, unlocking it and stepping inside.

Boss stepped inside the motel room only to be assaulted by a moldy smell. He shut the door behind him as he began looking around the small room. He walked over to the mid-sized bed and tossed his bags onto it. He then walked over to a half-shut door that he pushed open, and was surprised to see a decent-looking bathroom. He walked back to the bed, lay down, and let out a heavy sigh. He put his face in his hands, trying to get his thoughts together, only to hear his stomach growl loudly.

Boss ignored the growling from his stomach and continued with his thoughts until his stomach growled again but louder. He stood up from the bed and walked over to the room door, opened it, and stepped outside.

"Thought about my offer, handsome?" Boss heard, recognizing the voice even as he looked to his left to see the same light-skinned female who sat earlier on the stairwell with the white girl.

"Naw! I'm good, shorty!" Boss told the girl as he walked passed her.

"Where you going?" she asked him, looking over his muscular, toned, and still athletic body.

Boss stopped a few feet from where the girl stood inside one of the motel room's doorways.

He looked back over his shoulder at her and said, "Maybe you can help me out. Tell me where I can find something to eat?"

"Something to eat, huh?" she asked playfully, smiling flirtatiously at Boss before answering. "There's a Bar-B-Q Pit around the corner from here. They sell dinners out in front of the M&M's store."

"M&M's store?" Boss asked, with a look on his face.

Boss listened as shorty explained to him where the Bar-B-Q Pit was located. He then dug out his bankroll, peeled off a ten dollar bill, and then handed it over to the girl, nodding his head in thanks before turning and beginning to walk away.

* * *

Boss followed the female's directions and quickly smelled the barbecue in the air once he rounded the corner of the motel. He then started walking down the street after making a left at the corner and saw a crowd of cars, SUVs, and a few trucks. He made his way to the crowd of parked cars, only to see a huge mass of people either waiting in a long line or just standing around in a group talking, laughing, or smoking what he could smell was weed.

"Damn, baby! What's your name?" Boss heard as he was walked past a small crowd of three females.

He glanced in their direction but continued walking, looking in the direction in which the long line was facing. He saw two large barbecue grills and the two folded tables covered in red-and-white tablecloths that had what looked like cakes, pies, and all other types of food laid out on top of them.

Boss made the decision to first go inside the store, where he quickly noticed why the female back at the motel had called it M&M's, after seeing the big painted picture of the two yellow and red M&M's on the wall. He passed a crowd of four dudes, catching and ignoring the hard stares they were giving him as he walked inside.

* * *

Eazy was not surprised at all by the size of the crowd that was at the Bar-B-Q Pit, which his mother and father had been running for almost five years. Eazy slowed his Lexus LS 460, found a place to park, and turned the Lexus inside the open spot between a Mustang and a Nissan Maxima. Eazy shut off the car and climbed out of his Lexus. He locked the doors and started across the street, heading in the direction where his mother and father were working.

"What's up, Eazy?"

Eazy nodded to two fellas who called out to him and were posting with their ladies. He then nodded to a few more people who saw him and called out as he walked beside the two tables set up with the food on display.

"Erick! Hey, sweety!" Evelyn cried happily, after noticing her son and receiving a kiss on the cheek. "Where's Erica at?"

"I'm on the way over to her place now!" Eazy told his mother after speaking to his father. "Mom, you think you can make two dinners for me and Erica?"

"Sure, baby!" Evelyn answered while putting together a customer's plate.

Eazy told his mother and father that he would be right back

as he walked off and headed in the direction of the store. He first stopped to talk with two females who walked up on him, only for four guys to surround him out of nowhere.

"If it ain't the one and only Eazy himself," Lucky stated mockingly as he stepped up into Eazy's face. "I think we've got some unfinished business to handle, my nigga!"

"I already told you I ain't got shit for ya!" Eazy replied, causing Lucky to smile a mouthful of golds back at him.

"Let me make this a little easier," Lucky stated as he stepped nose to nose with Eazy. "I'm not asking you shit! I'm telling you it's either my way or I'ma deal with ya ass!"

"Man, whatever!" Eazy said as he turned to try to walk away, not wanting any trouble where both his parents worked.

Lucky grabbed his arm and jerked him back around to face him. "Muthafucker, you think this is some—!"

"Excuse me," Lucky and Eazy heard as a guy walked directly in between the two of them, forcing Lucky to release Eazy's arm.

"What the fuck!" Lucky barked, grabbing homeboy's arm and snatching him around. "Mutha!"

"First warning!" Homeboy spoke up in a calm but deadly toned voice, cutting off Lucky. "Get ya hand off me unless you trying to take it there."

Lucky opened his mouth to speak in response to what the guy in front of him had just said. But from the look in the young man's eyes, Lucky found himself releasing his arm and trying to save face. "I'ma let ya get a pass this time, youngin'! You better ask 'round about me."

"Yeah? I'll keep that in mind!" the guy replied, with a smirk while watching Lucky and his boys walk off.

"You're either crazy as hell or just careless as hell!" Eazy said with a smile, after witnessing what had just happened to Lucky in front of his boys.

"Who knows?" the guy replied, before shifting his eyes back to Lucky and his boys.

"What's ya name, my nigga?" Eazy asked him.

"Everybody calls me Boss!" he answered, looking back at Eazy.

After introducing himself, Eazy then asked Boss about where he was from, explaining that he noticed a southern accent.

"Atlanta!" Boss replied, before he nodded over to where Lucky was standing with his boys and a group of women. "What's up with that dude?"

"Who, Lucky?" Eazy said, looking over to where his crew all stood laughing.

"Dude really ain't shit! He just got put on with this nigga named Victor, and since then he's been doing some shit. He supposedly runs this area and has a spot in the apartments down the street from here."

"You say he supposedly runs this area?" Boss asked. "Doing what?"

"Selling weed, coke, and even pills . . . roxies!"

"You mean blues, right?"

"That's what everybody calls them."

Nodding his head, Boss looked back over at Lucky. "Tell me everything you can about that dude," Boss told Eazy.

"What you planning, my nigga?" Eazy asked, seeing the slow expression change on Boss's face.

\* \* \*

Lucky left the Bar-B-Q Pit after finally getting the phone call he was waiting for, which was why he was staying close by his main trap house. He then pulled the Escalade inside the parking lot at the Browns Apartment Complex, and he and his crew climbed from the truck after he parked.

After leaving the parking lot and entering the apartment building, Lucky led his crew upstairs just as his cell phone began to ring. He dug it out and saw that Victor's lieutenant, Prince, was calling.

Lucky answered the call while opening the apartment door. He stepped inside with his niggas following behind. He walked into the front room and hung up his phone after he finished up his call with Prince.

"Roc! Tony!" Lucky called out, looking over at his boys and noticing that Grip and Cash were missing. "Where the fuck did Grip and Cash go?"

"To handle something," Roc answered as he sat down on the sofa. "They said they'll be back."

"Whatever!" Lucky said. "Y'all go ahead and get that re-up money for this shit."

Lucky dropped onto the sofa as both Roc and Tony left the front room to collect the re-up. Lucky then snatched the TV remote and hit the power button to turn it on. But he was thinking back to the young-looking dude who was with soft-ass Eazy.

\* \* \*

"Let's make this shit quick!" Prince said to his back-up as the two of them climbed from the M3 BMW and started toward the entrance of the apartment building. "I ain't really trying to be out here dealing with this nigga Lucky longer than I have to."

Prince made his way up the front stairwell and walked up the hallway to Lucky's apartment. As Prince knocked on the door, he looked behind him at some dude walking past wearing a fitted cap. His attention was drawn back to the door, which was being unlocked and then swung open.

"Right on time!" Lucky said, seeing both Prince and his boy Murder Mike and motioning them inside the apartment.

"Be on point!" Prince whispered to Murder Mike. "I don't trust this nigga!"

Nodding his head as he and Prince stood in the front room, Murder Mike slid his right hand to his waist where his heater rested as Lucky entered the room.

"That's the work?" Lucky asked, nodding toward the two duffel bags that Prince held over his left and right shoulders.

"Where's the money at?" Prince asked at the same time Roc and Tony entered the room carrying a gray gym bag.

Lucky smiled at the sight of the gym bag, knowing exactly what was inside. He accepted the bag from Roc and then tossed it over at Prince's feet.

"There's your cash for ya, boss!"

Prince looked over at Murder Mike and nodded his head toward the gym bag as he waited for Mike to look inside and give a slight nod in return. Prince then tossed the two duffel bags to the floor beside Lucky as he turned to leave with Murder Mike following behind him.

Once they were both outside Lucky's apartment and walking down the hallway, Prince said, "I can't stand that nigga's ass! I don't understand why Victor even deals with that punk-ass muthafucker!"

"Probably, because the boy's a hustler," Murder Mike stated.

Prince shook his head as he and Murder Mike passed the same guy wearing the cap and leaning against the rail with a cigarette.

Once the two of them walked by the young man, Prince said, "That nigga ain't no fucking hustler. That shit Victor is giving his ass sells itself. It's that good! We can put a seven-year-old lil' nigga out there with that shit and that stuff is gonna move. You feel what I'm saying?"

Prince started down the stairwell but turned around when he did not hear Murder Mike respond to what he said. Prince paused in the middle section of the stairs after noticing Mike wasn't walking behind him.

"What the fuck!" Prince said, starting back up the stairwell.

He saw Mike's shoes a split second before pain exploded in his face and he felt himself falling backward down the stairs.

\* \* \*

Boss stepped over one of the guys he choked out and left sleeping on the ground. He then started down the stairwell behind the talkative guy carrying the gym bag, who he had seen enter the same apartment that belonged to Lucky, with two duffel bags.

Boss heard the pain from the moans homeboy was letting out, but he noticed the fucked-up way his body was twisted. Boss overlooked him and picked up the gym bag. He instantly felt the weight of the bag and unzipped it, and then he broke out in a smile after peeping inside and seeing it was filled with money.

"Happy damn birthday to a nigga!" Boss said, smiling as he zipped up the gym bag.

He then jogged back upstairs and started back in the direction of Lucky's apartment, holding the chrome .45 automatic he took from the homeboy out of sight at his thigh.

\* \* \*

"Go let them niggas in!" Lucky told Tony after hearing the knocking at the apartment door while he, Roc, and Tony were looking over what was sent to them by Victor.

Once Tony left the bedroom and went to answer the front door, Lucky turned his full attention to the work laid out in front of him.

"A'ight! Let's get this shit put up, and we'll get this shit spread out to everyone tomorrow morning after breaking this shit down."

Lucky packed everything back inside the two duffel bags and realized Tony was still missing.

"Go and see what the fuck is taking that fool Tony so long," Lucky instructed Roc.

"Relax!" both Lucky and Roc heard, looking up just as a bloody-faced Tony stumbled back into the room and fell at their feet.

Lucky looked up from his boy, whose face was fucked up and looked like somebody had stomped it in. He then locked up stiff once his eyes met the same golden-green gaze he saw earlier at the Bar-B-Q Pit.

*Boom! Boom! Boom!*

Lucky jumped each time the gun went off in the young man's hand. He looked down at himself and saw no blood or holes. However, he turned around just in time to see Roc sliding slowly down the wall to the floor with three holes in his chest, leaving a bloody trail down the wall.

"Happy to see me, playboy?" Boss asked as he walked farther into the bedroom, stepped over the guy who answered the front door, and stopped in front of Lucky. "I'm pretty happy to see you, and I even took your advice and looked into who you was."

"Dawg, you ain't gotta—!"

"Those for me, right?" Boss asked, nodding toward the bed where the two duffel bags were sitting.

"Come on, man!" Lucky cried as he started toward Boss, only to freeze once he came face to face with the barrel of the .45 Boss now had pointed at his face. "Man, come on! This shit don't belong to me!"

"Two decisions!" Boss stated, staring hard and straight into Lucky's eyes. "Either back the fuck up and lay your bitch ass down on the ground, or end up like your boy behind you!"

"Dawg, come on!"

*Boom!*

Boss watched as Lucky's body stumbled backward after blowing a hole in the clown's face. Boss then turned and snatched up the two duffel bags. He heard the sound of Lucky's body hitting the ground just as he was rushing out of the bedroom.

## THREE

**BOSS LEFT LUCKY'S APARTMENT** and his nosey neighbors who wanted to know what was going on. He first stopped back at his room and grabbed his bags, and then dropped off his room key at the front desk with the white guy who was still staring at the small television. He then wasted no time leaving the motel, heading in the direction opposite the Bar-B-Q Pit.

Boss stepped out onto the corner of the main street. He first looked up the street and then down the street in the opposite direction and saw a 7-Eleven store. He started in that direction. Once he entered the parking lot a few minutes later, he saw a bank of three pay phones at the end of the storefront. Boss first walked into the store and grabbed a bottle of water from the refrigerator. He paid for it with a five-dollar bill, and asked for his change to be in coins.

Once he was back outside, Boss walked directly to the pay phones. He noticed that two of them were broken, so he reached for the third phone. He picked up the handset and heard a dial tone, and then he deposited some coins and called for a cab.

After hanging up, he stood back, leaned against the wall with a cigarette, and gripped his .45 with his right hand in the front of his jeans. Once he saw the taxi finally pull into the 7-Eleven, he stepped out toward the car as it pulled up and stopped in front of him.

"Where are we going, sir?" the cab driver asked his new passenger.

"Take me to a hotel somewhere else!" Boss told the driver, after shutting the back door and then setting his bags to his left on the seat.

Boss sat back and sighed as he looked out the window as the taxi driver drove off and away from the 7-Eleven. He thought back to what had just happened only a little while ago, and saw the entire scene play out again inside his mind.

* * *

Boss was deep in thought when the cab driver began slowing and turning into the parking lot of a hotel. He lost his train of thought once the taxi cab stopped and the driver called back to him announcing their arrival at the new motel.

Boss stared out the window at the tall hotel and nodded his head in approval, comparing it to the motel from which he had just left. He then passed the cab driver what he owed him, grabbed his bags, and climbed from inside the cab.

After the cab pulled off, Boss headed toward the front entrance to the hotel. He opened the door as two women and a little girl exited the lobby. When he walked inside, the lobby was surprisingly empty. Boss approached the registration and saw a white, red-headed woman behind the front desk. He asked for a room for three weeks' time, explaining that he wanted a room overlooking the parking lot.

After Boss paid for the hotel room, he received a key card. He thanked the smiling white woman at the desk and then headed over to the elevator. After a few moments, he stepped onto the elevator once the doors had opened.

Once he arrived on the fifth floor, Boss stepped off and walked up the hallway in search of his hotel room. Boss stopped in front of his door and placed his key card into the slot to unlock the door. He stepped inside the room and hit the light switch he saw on the wall on this right. Once the room lit up, he shut the door behind him.

Boss quickly saw the difference in the size and condition of the room compared to the motel room. He walked over to the large bed and tossed all five bags onto it. He then pushed his own duffel bag and backpack off to the side and grabbed one of Lucky's men's duffel bags. He opened it and broke out in a huge smile at what he saw. Grabbing the second duffel bag and opening it made him smile even more.

"This shit can't be for real!" Boss stated as he began emptying out both duffel bags.

He stood up and stared down at what was five pounds of White Rhino weed, which he recognized from its whitish color, as well as four bricks of cocaine and two extra-large ziplock bags filled with blue pills he knew as roxies.

Boss shook his head and smiled. He then reached for the gym bag and opened it, which revealed cash inside. He dumped out all the money onto the bed and then tossed the bag to the side before turning his attention back to the pile of cash.

"This shit can't be serious!" he said as he began counting.

* * *

"This is what the fuck I'm talking about!" Boss stated, smiling a huge grin after counting the money from the hit off Lucky and his people, and coming up with a total of $250,000.

Boss stood up from the bed and stared down at the drugs and money all over the bed. He got control of the many thoughts that were flowing through his mind. He then dug out his Newports as he left the bed and walked over to the room window. After opening it, he lit up a cigarette that he removed from the pack, took a deep pull, and then blew out the smoke, watching as it floated out the window.

"This is my chance!" Boss said to himself after coming to the decision that not only was he not going to return to Atlanta, but he'd remain in Miami and build up his own empire.

Boss finished his cigarette but left the window open. He walked back to the bed and began packing the money back into the gym bag. After that he packed the weed, pills, and cocaine back into the two duffel bags. Boss then lay out across the bed, pulling the .45 from his waist and laying it at his side on his right. He closed his eyes to think and rest for a while.

# FOUR

**BOSS WAS UNSURE OF** exactly the time he fell asleep that night, but he was awakened by the sounds of loud laughing coming from out in the hallway. He remained lying across the bed a little while longer still getting his mind together, and finally climbed out of bed and headed to the bathroom.

After using the toilet and washing his face, he returned to the bed. Boss grabbed what he needed for the shower and then headed back inside the bathroom. After spending about six minutes in the shower, he got out, dried off, and looked at himself in the mirror, seeing that he needed a haircut and a trim-up.

He left the bathroom and returned to the bed area after putting on his Ralph Lauren boxers and black Ralph Lauren wifebeater. Boss then picked out a Polo outfit and some all-white Air Force Ones.

After dressing, Boss grabbed his backpack and emptied it. He put on a gray-over-white Yankees cap and then grabbed the other bag and counted out $50,000 and stuffed it inside his backpack, with the intentions of taking care of business as far as setting up business and looking for a nice place to live somewhere. Boss put away the rest of his things and then grabbed both his backpack and the .45 from the bed as he made his way to the door.

He rode the elevator down to the lobby and stopped at the front desk. He asked the white male desk clerk to call him a taxi as he walked outside to await its arrival.

Boss lit up another Newport and went over his plans once more, still feeling as if there was something that wasn't right about everything he was putting together inside his head. He saw the taxi cab turn into the hotel parking lot, so he tossed down the butt as he started walking over to the cab.

"Where we going?" the cab driver asked.

"I'm trying to find a good used car dealership," Boss told the driver, planning to start things off first with finding some wheels and not having to deal with calling a taxi every time he wanted to go somewhere.

* * *

The driver took Boss to three dealerships after leaving the hotel; however, Boss turned down everything he was shown. Boss was riding in the back seat of the taxi and heading to a final dealership, when something caught his eye.

"Whoa!" Boss cried out to the cab driver, looking through the back windshield. "Turn around!"

"Excuse me?" the driver asked, looking at his passenger in his rear-view mirror.

"Turn the fuck around!" Boss barked, and shot his driver a look.

The driver quickly turned the taxi cab around as he was told.

Boss turned his attention back to a car he spotted that was parked in front of a royal blue and white house. He turned in his seat and directed the cab driver where they were going. Boss smiled as they pulled up alongside the familiar 2009 Porsche Twin Turbo that was a pearl-black color with dark tinted windows that had a For Sale sign in the window.

After paying the cab driver, Boss grabbed his backpack and climbed out from inside the cab. He walked over to the Porsche, smiling as he looked over the car.

"Can I help you, sir?" a voice called out.

Boss looked behind him after hearing the question and saw an older-looking white guy who was perhaps in his mid-thirties with short black hair.

"Good morning. I was wondering if you're still selling the Porsche?" Boss said as he walked over to the gate.

"You interested?" the white guy asked.

"Yes, sir!" Boss respectfully answered.

"Hold on there! Let me go get the keys, and I'll be with you," the white guy told Boss, before disappearing back inside the house.

Boss waited a few minutes until the owner reappeared. He also noticed a blonde white woman who followed the man to the door and was staring directly at him. Boss then shifted his gaze back to the guy as he stepped out of the gate.

"How old are you, if you don't mind me asking?" the guy inquired as he walked around to the driver's door of the Porsche.

"I'm nineteen!" Boss answered truthfully as he followed the guy to the driver's door.

He unlocked and opened up the car door, and then motioned to the young man to have a seat inside.

"Are you also expecting your father or mother to come soon to look at the car?"

"How much?" Boss asked, ignoring the question he was just asked.

"I'm asking $25,000 for it!" he told Boss. "The car is in mint condition and drives smoothly. I've even had brand-new tires put on it as well."

Boss nodded his head as he listened to what the man told him. He then looked at the navigation system and said,

"Alright. I'll take it!"

"You'll take it?" the white man asked. "You mean you're interested in buying it?"

"Naw!" Boss answered as he opened his backpack and pulled out a handful of money.

Boss also heard the surprised sound the man made beside him after seeing the money in his hand.

\* \* \*

Boss pulled off in front of the white guy's house, who he found out was named Ted. Boss then leaned back inside his seashell leather interior driver's seat, steering the Porsche with his left hand and smiling. He couldn't believe he was actually driving a Porsche, since it was his favorite car.

He then continued his day's plan and pulled up to a T-Mobile store. He bought a new iPhone 7 and allowed the saleswoman to talk him into buying a black leather phone case. He also accepted her phone number after she told him to give her a call.

After leaving the T-Mobile store and finding a shopping center a few minutes later, Boss noticed a barber shop. He parked the Porsche beside a white Aston Martin V12 Vantage, shut off the engine, and climbed out.

\* \* \*

"Oh shit!" Maxine cried, grabbing her roommate and best friend. She pointed to the door just as the guy she was staring at walked inside the beauty parlor/barber shop. "Bitch, look at his ass! He is too fine!"

"Maxine, let me go!" Brandi told her girl, pulling away from her.

She looked in the direction Maxine was pointing, only to lock eyes with the guy with the white fitted cap staring straight at her—or was he?

"Girl, he's looking at you!" Maxine cried with excitement.

The young man entered the shop staring at Brandi, but suddenly looked away and walked toward one of the barbers. Brandi continued watching the guy even as he was talking with her cousin, Tim. She was still watching him when Maxine yelled out her name, getting her attention.

"Yeah?"

"Erica's ready for you. Go!" Maxine told Brandi, smiling after catching Miss I Ain't Got Time for Niggas.

Brandi stood up from her seat but glanced back over to the guy still talking with Tim. She walked over to her friend and hairdresser to get her hair washed and set, but she was definitely going to go over to talk to her cousin and get a closer look at Mr. Handsome.

* * *

Boss waited a little over ten minutes before he finally got to sit in the barber's chair. He explained how he wanted his hair cut and how he wanted his chin-strap beard edge with a razor as well as his tape line. Boss sat relaxing inside the seat with his eyes closed, listening to the Rick Ross song that his barber, Tim, had playing on the stereo system behind him on a glass table.

"Yo, Tim!" Boss called out to the barber.

"Yeah!"

"Where's the mall at around here?"

"Mall, huh?" Tim asked, looking down at the young-looking dude who introduced himself as Boss. "You ain't from around here, are ya youngin'?"

"I'm from Atlanta!" Boss admitted. "I just moved here last night."

"You new on Miami then?"

"Pretty much."

"We got a few malls," Tim told Boss as he began to give him locations and directions.

Once Tim finished talking, and after a brief moment, Boss asked, "You smoke, big homie?"

"Smoke what?" Tim asked, looking down at Boss.

"Weed!" Boss answered quickly, deciding that if Tim was into smoking, then he would slowly work homeboy into spreading the word about him.

"You selling some?" Tim asked.

"Yeah!" Boss answered. "You trying to cop some? It's that White Rhino."

"Yeah? I'ma get some off you!" Tim told Boss. "What you selling?"

"You know what you want?"

"How about an ounce?"

"It's $500 an ounce."

"Yeah! I'm a fuck with that, youngin'," Tim said with a smile. "You got it on you or what?"

"After I leave here, I'll get that and come back through with it!" Boss explained to Tim.

\* \* \*

Brandi paid Erica once her hair was done and then promised to call her later. She started straight for her cousin, Tim, hearing Maxine call out her name while she was still sitting in her chair. Brandi ignored Maxine and continued walking in her cousin's direction.

"Tim!" Brandi called out, walking up on her cousin.

"What's up, Brandi?" Tim said, kissing his baby cousin's cheek. "You still here?"

"I'm waiting on Maxine," Brandi admitted. "Tim, what happened to that guy you had over here earlier?"

"Which one?" he asked, looking from the customer's head inside his seat to his cousin.

"The white fitted cap guy with the metallic blue jeans and white Air Force Ones."

"You mean the young nigga Boss?"

"Who?"

"Boss!" Tim repeated. "He goes by Boss."

"Boss?" Brandi asked again, before she said, "What's his real name?"

"He ain't say," Tim answered before he paused and looked at his cousin. "Hold up! Why you so interested in homeboy?"

"Don't worry about it!" Brandi answered as she started to walk off.

"He's coming back through though!" Tim announced.

Turning back to face her cousin, Brandi asked, "He's coming back for real, Tim?"

"That's what he said," Tim answered truthfully. "He's supposed to bring me something back here."

Brandi nodded her head and smiled as she turned and walked off.

## FIVE

**BOSS RETURNED TO THE** hotel after first picking up a few things at a Walmart he found. He sat at the hotel weighing out an ounce of weed and even bagged up a few twenty-dollar sacks. He then left the hotel and made the drive back over to the shopping center where the barber shop was located.

He turned into the parking lot and pulled up in front of the shop. Boss then dug out his cell phone and hit up Tim's number he had programmed inside his iPhone.

"Yo!" Tim answered on the start of the third ring.

"What's up, playboy? This is Boss!"

"What's up, youngin'? Where you at?"

"I'm outside, my nigga. Come on outside real quick!"

"I'm on my way."

Boss hung up the phone and then tossed it inside the center console. He picked up the rolled blunt he put together, lit it, and then quickly smelled the strong weed smell and felt its strength. He held in the smoke a few moments, and then slowly blew it out.

Boss hit the blunt again, just as he saw Tim step out of the shop. He let down the window and called out to Tim, waving him over to his car.

"What's up, youngin'?" Tim said after walking up to the driver's seat.

"Get in!" Boss told him, hitting the locks as Tim walked around the car and climbed into the Porsche.

"That's you right there," Tim said as he tossed the brown paper bag into Tim's lap.

Tim opened the bag and removed the plastic-wrapped ounce of weed. Tim broke out in a smile as he then dug out the

$500 he had set to the side for Boss and handed it to him.

"Good looking art, youngin'!"

"Smoke with me!" Boss said, handing over his blunt to Tim.

Tim took a pull from the blunt and instantly began coughing and choking. He tried talking, but he had to finish coughing.

"Yo! This is the same shit you just gave me?"

Boss nodded his head and smirked. "Tell your people that's looking for some to get at me. You got my number," Boss told him.

"I got you, youngin'," Tim stated, dapping up with Boss, only to spot both his cousin and Maxine stepping out of the shop. "Yeah! I almost forgot, youngin'. My cousin was asking about you, too."

"Your cousin?"

"Her name is Brandi. That's her right there."

Boss looked outside his window at whom Tim was pointing. Boss slowly began smirking after quickly recognizing the shorty he had seen earlier.

"Call her?" Boss asked.

Tim climbed out of the Porsche and called out to Brandi, waving over to him.

* * *

Brandi left Maxine at the Aston Martin and walked over to the Porsche, where she saw Tim climb out and walk around to meet her. Brandi then stopped in front of Tim.

"Who that?" she asked, nodding at the Porsche.

"It's who you wanted!" Tim told his cousin.

He then tapped on the window before walking off and leaving Brandi standing in front of the Porsche.

Brandi watched Tim as he walked off, but looked back at the Porsche just as the driver's door opened and the same guy she was waiting for stepped out of the car. She instantly began smiling at the simple sight of him.

"What's up, shorty?" Boss said, smiling at her. "You wanted to see me, ma?"

"Who told you I wanted to see you?" Brandi asked still smiling. "I only asked what your name was!"

"Well, it's Boss!"

"Boss, huh?"

"Pretty much!"

"So that's what your mother named you?"

"Naw! She named me ReSean, but I'm known as Boss though. What's your name?" he said with a smile.

"Why you wanna know?" she asked, folding her arms across her C-cup perky breasts, catching his eyes lowering to her breasts and then back to her eyes.

"How am I supposed to know what to call you when I hit your phone up later?"

"Who told you I was giving you my number to call?"

"I'm asking," he told her, stepping closer to her perfectly built and curvy but thick and soft-looking five foot two, 139-pound, and 34-27-43 frame, which caused shorty to lift her eyes higher to look into his eyes.

"You gonna let your man call you later, right?"

"My man?" Brandi asked, speaking in a softer voice. "I don't have one of those, Boss."

"Now you do!" he told her. "Or am I wrong about what I'm getting from your vibe?"

"You're not wrong!" Brandi answered truthfully. "My name's Brandi, but if you're trying to talk to me later, then I wanna see you later too."

"Whatever you want, shorty," Boss said, smiling as he opened the car door and leaned inside to get his cell phone.

Brandi exchanged numbers with Boss and stood talking with him a little longer until Maxine started to rush her.

"When you calling me, ReSean?" Brandi asked before saying goodbye.

"I'm about to handle something real quick, but I'ma hit you up afterward," Boss informed her as a Lexus slowly pulled up beside him and Brandi.

He stood staring at the car.

"Shorty, you know who that is?" he asked.

"That's my girl Erica's man!" Brandi answered as she turned and started toward the Lexus, only for the driver's window to slide down and a smiling Eazy to sit staring out of the car.

"If it ain't that Atlanta nigga, Boss!" Eazy said, smiling when he recognized the young dude from the other night at the Bar-B-Q Pit. "I see you move fast, my nigga."

"Eazy!" Boss said, smiling now that he also recognized the other man from last night.

He started toward the Lexus as Eazy was climbing out of the car.

"Wait a minute!" Brandi said, looking from Boss to Eazy and back as the two of them embraced in a brotherly hug. "You two know each other?"

"We met last night," Eazy answered. "I got into a lil' something, and Boss was there to help me out with it."

"Well, damn!" Brandi said smiling as she looked back at

Boss. "Well, I'ma let you hang with your boy, but I expect to get a call from you soon because I do expect to see you later."

"I got you, shorty!" Boss told Brandi, winking his eye at her and smirking.

"Whoa!" Eazy cried in disbelief. He stared at Brandi and asked, "You mean you already kicking it with my nigga Boss?"

"Mind your business, Eazy!" Brandi told him playfully, rolling her eyes as she turned around, walked away, and headed over to her car where Maxine was waiting.

"Girl! I wanna know everything!" Maxine cried as soon as Brandi was inside of the Aston Martin.

* * *

After Brandi drove off inside her Aston Martin with a smile and a wave goodbye to him, Boss focused his attention on Eazy, who instantly mentioned what had happened with Lucky and somebody named Prince.

"Who the hell is this Prince dude?" Boss asked as he leaned back against the Porsche and folded his arms across his chest.

"Homeboy with the scar on his neck on the left side," Eazy told Boss. "They found him and his boy, Murder Mike, fucked up on the stairwell at Lucky's apartment, and they found Lucky with most of his face missing, and both his niggas, Roc and Tony, dead beside him. I wonder how that shit happened?"

"Who knows?" Boss replied, smirking as he stood staring at a smiling Eazy.

"Fuck 'em!" Eazy stated, with a wave of the hand. "That's less problems for me! What's up though? What you about to get into?"

"I was headed to the mall and then probably to do a little

networking."

"Networking?"

"I just so happen to have come up on some stuff I'm trying to get off, and at the same time, I wanna build my network up. You feeling what I'm saying?"

"No doubt!" Eazy answered. "What all you working with though?"

"Right now I'm just messing 'round with the weed I'm holding, but my real focus is on moving these pills and this coke I'm sitting on."

"You may have a hard time with that!" Eazy told him. He then explained, "There's only two niggas that's really controlling the coke game around the city, and that's this nigga Malcolm White Jr., and then you've got that fool Dollar Bill. But it's his brother, Victor Murphy, who's out there pushing his shit, and that's who Lucky was working for before the clown got bodied by some nigga nobody knows."

"You say this nigga Malcolm White and some dude named Dollar Bill are really running the coke game down here, huh?"

"Pretty much!"

"So, what you pushing?"

Eazy smiled at the young nigga's question, but caught good vibes from him.

"I push pills and roxies, Percocet, and even some lean," Eazy told him.

"Lean?" Boss repeated. "What the fuck is that?"

"It's really just codeine and promethazine mixed together," Eazy explained. "I really just started fucking with it because of my friend Rico. He got me selling that shit with him."

Boss nodded his head after listening to Eazy, and then said, "I may have a new idea, but I may need your help. You got me?"

"Let me slide up in this shop and holla at my lady real quick; then we can roll out," Eazy told Boss before hopping back inside the Lexus and parking the car.

\* \* \*

Boss met Eazy's lady, Erica, before the two of them left the barber/beauty shop. Boss followed behind Eazy as he showed him around and took Boss to two different stores to pick up the things he needed. Afterward, both of them drove out to the Aventura Mall, where Boss did some shopping and Eazy picked up a few things as well. They left the mall after a few hours, and Boss stopped and picked up something to eat before leading Eazy to his hotel.

"This you?" Eazy asked, after parking the Lexus and walking over to Boss's car to help with the bags.

"Yeah!" Boss answered, handing Eazy a few bags and then grabbing the others from the trunk.

He shut the trunk and then led the way across the parking lot into the hotel. They took the elevator to Boss's floor and then his room. Boss used his key card to unlock the door and then pushed open the door. After locking it, he and Eazy walked over to his bed.

"Just toss those bags on the floor against the walls," Boss asked Eazy as he set down the bags with the stuff he bought at Bed, Bath & Beyond and the smoke shop Eazy took him.

Boss grabbed the two duffel bags with the weed, cocaine, and pills inside, and set both bags on top of the bed.

"You working or watching?" Boss said to Eazy as he looked over at him.

"I'm here, so I may as well help out!" Eazy told him, but added with a smile, "But you gonna owe me for this."

"I got you!" Boss stated.

He then turned his attention to the two duffel bags, from which he took out one of the four bricks of cocaine and one of the freezer-size XL ziplock bags filled with pills. He motioned to Eazy to grab the bags and follow behind him.

Once they were inside the sitting area in front of a wooden coffee table, Boss set down the brick and the bag of pills. He then motioned for Eazy to hand him the bags, before he sat down in the couch-like seat.

"What exactly are you about to do?" Eazy asked, sitting across from Boss and watching him as he pulled out the scale, four boxes of pill capsules, and a few other things he bought.

"Tell me something!" Boss asked Eazy as he tossed him some latex gloves. "What are the effects of roxies, or blues as they're called, once you take them?"

"I don't fuck with 'em, but from what I see, they have people in a lazy kind of relaxed state almost like heroin," Eazy explained.

"Alright! So what does coke do to you when you take it?" Boss asked while opening up one of the pill case boxes.

"I know that shit is a stimulant and be having muthafuckers wilding the fuck out after they come down from their high," Eazy explained. "Why you asking these questions? What's really up, my nigga?"

Boss stopped what he was doing with the ziplock bag full of roxies. He then sat back in his seat and dug out one of Newports.

"What do you think will happen when a depressant drug like roxie, which is a synthetic heroin, and a stimulant drug like cocaine are mixed together?"

"Hold up! Wait!" Eazy said, holding up both hands as he was beginning to understand. "You telling me you're about to mix coke and roxies together and push that shit out on the streets?"

"Pretty much!" Boss answered with a small smile. "I'ma call it blue devils."

"Blue devils, huh?" Eazy repeated while slowly smiling because he actually liked the name.

## SIX

**BOSS AND EAZY WERE** unsure exactly how long the two of them actually had been at work breaking down the bricks of cocaine and the roxies, mixing, weighing, and then filling the capsules with the cocaine and roxie combination. They both sat smoking blunts and talking, when, first, Eazy's phone went off, followed by Boss's phone. They grabbed their phones off the coffee table, and Boss looked down at the screen and saw that Brandi was calling him.

Boss finished up the capsule he was filling with the mixture and then picked up his phone. He placed it between his right shoulder and ear.

"What's up, shorty?" he answered.

"Don't what's up me, ReSean!" Brandi cried, upset. "Why haven't you called me? I told you I wanted to see you later, and it's already three o'clock. Where are you?"

"I know you better mind how you calling and getting on a nigga's ass about not hitting you up on time!" Boss started playfully, but then added, "Relax though, ma. I ain't forgot about you, shorty. I'm just handling a little business with Eazy right now."

"You still with Eazy's ass?"

"Yeah, why?"

"Because his girlfriend's with me right now and is going off on his ass now too!"

Looking over at Eazy and seeing his boy's facial expression, Boss said into the phone: "Shorty, where y'all at now?"

"We about to get something to eat at the Bar-B-Q Pit. Why?"

"We're on our way!" Boss told her.

He then hung up the phone, began cleaning up the rest of the mix, and put away the scale and the rest of the equipment.

"Bruh! What's up?" Eazy asked, after finally hanging up with his lady.

"Brandi called!" Boss told him. "We about to meet up with Brandi and your lady, but at the same time, I'ma start pushing this blue devil and see how it sells. Let's get this shit put up and get outta here!"

\* \* \*

Boss and Eazy left the hotel together inside his Porsche and drove back across town, making it to the Bar-B-Q Pit a short while later and seeing the same type of crowd. Boss slowed his car and saw Brandi's Aston Martin, and parked beside it.

"Damn, sexy!" a redbone female called out as she stood with two of her girls staring at the driver of the Porsche Twin Turbo. "What's your name, baby?"

"Taken!" Brandi answered as she and Erica walked up.

She walked straight up to Boss, only to stop directly in front of him and fold her arms across her chest.

"What was you doing that took so long, ReSean?"

"Why? You miss me, ma?" Boss asked, smirking down at her, only to cause her to smile and roll her eyes playfully at him.

"You eating with us, right?"

"We already ate, but I'm down for some ribs though!" Boss stated as both Eazy and Erica walked over to join him and Brandi.

"Hey, Boss!" Erica said, smiling at him.

"What's up, Erica?" Boss said.

Boss winked at her, and at the same time, he dug out a knot of money from his pocket, peeled off a twenty, and handed it over to Brandi. "That's for our food. You want something from outta the store?"

"Just something to drink," Brandi replied.

She smiled as she stood watching him and Eazy walk off toward the store.

"Girl, from the way you staring at Boss, I'ma start thinking you already feeling that man!" Erica stated, smiling as Brandi turned to look at her.

"I don't know, Erica!" Brandi said as she and Erica started toward the Bar-B-Q Pit. "There's something about that boy."

"You mean other than the fact that his ass is drop-dead gorgeous?" Erica said as the both of them began laughing and high-fiving in agreement.

* * *

Boss exited the store after buying two drinks and a box of cognac-flavored blunt wraps. He then followed Eazy outside, only to pause as a young-looking homeless guy rushed up to Eazy.

Boss opened up the Corona he just bought and then listened to the homeless guy beg Eazy for either something to smoke or a few dollars. Boss then heard Eazy call the guy Berry and tell him that he didn't have anything on him.

"You looking to try something new, playboy?" Boss spoke up asking the homeless guy.

"You got something, main man?" Berry asked, walking up on Boss, who calmly stepped back a step.

"I tell you what, playboy! I'ma let you try something new! It's called a blue devil. You like it, I want you to come back and find me before I leave; and if you bring me some more customers, I'll take care of you, alright?" Boss told the guy while digging out one of the pills from inside of a baggy.

"What's this?" Berry asked, looking down at the pill he held inside his hand.

"You don't want it?" Eazy asked, reaching for the pill.

Snatching the pill away from Eazy, Berry backed away, but looked to Boss and said, "I'll let you know, Boss man! If it's good, Berry will let you know."

Eazy shook his head and smiled as he watched Berry run off with the pill that Boss had just given him.

Eazy looked to Boss and said, "You just gave that blue devil to the right muthafucker. If you wanna muthafucker to know about your shit, Berry Young is gonna spread the word!"

"That's what I'm hoping for!" Boss replied as he and Eazy started toward the girls who stood talking with both of Eazy's parents.

"There goes my baby," Evelyn cried, happy to see her son, and smiling as Eazy walked over and kissed her on the cheek.

She then noticed Boss, remembered his name, and said, "How are you doing, ReSean, sweety?"

"I'm doing fine, Mrs. Collins," Boss replied as he hugged Eazy's mother and then shook hands with a busy Darrell Collins.

"ReSean, here!" Brandi said, walking up to Boss and handing him his plate of food. "Mrs. Collins remembered what you liked from last night."

"ReSean, why didn't you tell me you were seeing my goddaughter?" Evelyn asked Boss as she was taking care of another customer.

"Goddaughter?" Boss asked, with a confused look on his face.

"Brandi, ReSean!" Evelyn introduced Boss while smiling at the gorgeous young man. "She's my goddaughter. Her mother is my oldest and best friend, sweety."

"I didn't know she—!"

"Yo, Eazy!" Boss heard in mid-sentence.

He recognized the aggression in the way Eazy's name was yelled, so he turned around to see two guys walking straight toward his friend.

"Erick!" Evelyn cried in worry, seeing the two young men with angry expressions on their faces.

"I'm okay!" Eazy told her, recognizing that it was Lucky's two boys, Grip and Cash.

"Erick!" Evelyn cried out to her son as he walked off to meet with the two guys.

"I'll go with him, Mrs. Collins," Boss spoke up to Evelyn as he followed behind and walked up beside his boy.

As the two guys were talking real aggressively, Boss interrupted: "Eazy, what's up? Everything good, playboy?"

"Nigga! I remember you!" Cash said, staring Boss up and down. "You the punk-ass nigga that talked that gangsta shit the other night."

"Look, fellas," Eazy spoke up, "I just told y'all and I'ma gonna say it one more time. I don't know who murdered ya man Lucky."

"I heard about that shit too!" Boss said, drawing both Cash's and Grip's attention back to him. "I heard the nigga Lucky ran into some real gangster dude that up and opened his melon."

"Oh, you think shit's funny, huh?" Grip asked, stepping up into Boss's face.

Remaining calm but with a deadly serious expression, Boss said, "I won't go back and forth with you about that nigga Lucky being killed, but I can promise that if you act up out here, you will end up just like your boy Lucky! Be sure of your next decision, because if it's the wrong one, you will not get a second chance."

"Mutha—!"

"Grip, come on!" Cash spoke up, cutting off his boy and grabbing his arm.

Boss watched as Grip and Cash walked off and whispered to themselves.

He then looked over to Eazy and said, "I'ma have to deal with them two fools!"

"I was thinking the same exact thing!" Eazy said as he and Boss started back over to where the others stood waiting and watching.

"Is everything okay?" Erica asked as Eazy and Boss stepped back within the group.

"Everything's straight," Eazy told his lady, dropping his arm around her waist and pulling Erica up against him, causing her to smile and throw her arm around his neck.

Boss smiled while watching the two of them as he looked over at Evelyn and saw her smile too. He read her lips as she thanked him.

* * *

Boss and Eazy chilled with Erica, Brandi, Evelyn, and Darrell as business began to slow but never stop at the Bar-B-

Q Pit. Both Boss and Eazy were caught up laughing at something Mrs. Collins said, when Boss heard his name.

"Boss, you got company!" Eazy told him, smiling as he nodded to the crowd of what looked like ten people being led by a stumbling Berry.

"ReSean, who's that?" Brandi asked as she stood leaned up against him. She then turned back and stared at the crowd heading in their direction.

"I'll be right back," Boss told the others, leaving Brandi staring at him walking off.

"Erick, what's going on?" Evelyn asked her son while watching Boss with the group of women and men.

"He's talking with them, Momma!" Eazy told her as he looked over and saw a crowd begin surrounding Boss.

Brandi watched Boss and caught on to what he was up to as she walked over to Eazy and Erica.

"Eazy, what's ReSean selling?" Brandi asked in a lowered voice.

"Weed!" Eazy lied.

"So, you just gonna lie now, Eazy?" Brandi asked, placing her hands on her wide and curvy hips while staring at him. "Berry don't smoke nothing but crack!"

"Well, he ain't selling—!"

*Thraaah! Thraaah! Thraaah!*

Eazy ducked at the sound of rapid machine gun fire, pulling down both Erica and Brandi with him. Eazy looked over and saw his father pull down his mother as the rapid firing continued.

"Stay down!" Eazy yelled to his lady and Brandi, before running to see Boss take off in the opposite direction.

Eazy pulled out his 9mm and followed in the direction Boss

went. He could hear the canon-like sound ringing out and saw Boss standing in the middle of the street holding a chrome .45 automatic.

"Boss, what's up?" Eazy yelled, running up beside him. "Who the fuck you banging at, bruh?"

"I knew I should have deaded them clowns!" Boss said as he and Eazy jogged back over to the parking lot.

Once Boss and Eazy returned with the girls and Mr. and Mrs. Collins, they explained that they needed to go but would call them later. Eazy kissed both his mother and Erica goodbye, and he saw the worried look on his mother's face and the questioning look on Erica's. Boss kissed Brandi and then kissed Mrs. Collins's cheek, before he and Eazy jogged off across the street and headed to his Porsche.

"Who the fuck was that you were busting at?" Eazy asked, once he and Boss were inside the car and Boss had the Porsche flying out of the spot and speeding down the street.

"Where them clowns be at that was just out here at the Pit talking about that nigga Lucky?" Boss asked while speeding away from the Bar-B-Q Pit.

"You talking about Grip's and Cash's nigga asses?" Eazy asked. "I know the nigga Cash gotta sister who dances at the same club where Brandi dances. We can go and holla at her if you really trying to find them niggas, because I'm pretty sure we won't be finding them fools by ourselves."

"Fuck it!" Boss said. "Where's this club at?"

* * *

Swinging the Porsche inside the parking lot at the Pink Palace and ignoring the crowd and not bothering to park, Boss stopped the car in front of the club's entrance. Then both he and Eazy climbed from the Porsche.

"Yo! Y'all can't park there!" the security guard at the front door called out to Boss and Eazy, only for Boss to pull out some money and toss it to him.

"Watch my shit!" Boss told the security guard as he and Eazy entered the strip club bypassing the line and leaving the security guard staring with a stupid look on his face.

Once inside the two-story club and seeing that it was even more crowded, Eazy looked around and tried to spot Cash's sister while Boss stepped over to the bar to get the bartender's attention.

"Yo, Eazy!" Boss called him over. "What's shorty's name?"

"They call her Strawberry," Eazy answered.

Boss turned back to the bartender and repeated the name to him, and received information where she was.

Boss then turned back to Eazy and said, "Shorty's upstairs."

After leaving the bar, Boss and Eazy headed for the stairs to find Strawberry.

\* \* \*

Pleasure was unsure of who she had just seen, but she was pretty certain it was who she thought it was from the smooth way he walked. She left the guy she had been talking with and walked over to the bar and called out to the bartender.

"Hey, Pleasure, girl!" the bartender yelled over the music. "What's up?"

"Who was the guy you was just talking to—the one with

the fitted cap?"

"He didn't say his name, but he was looking for Strawberry, and his ass was fine as hell with them green eyes."

"Green eyes?" Pleasure asked.

"Yes, girl. They were like a green with a little golden brown in them," the bartender told Pleasure with a smile, remembering the guy's eyes.

Pleasure looked back in the direction of her friend the bartender, who sounded interested in the guy she was describing. She then asked him where Strawberry was. After finding out, she started for the stairs that led up to the second level of the club.

* * *

As soon as they entered the upstairs VIP area, Eazy spotted Strawberry and pointed her out to Boss. She was dancing for a dark-skinned clown with too much gold and too many gold teeth. Both Eazy and Boss walked straight over to her.

"Strawberry!" Boss said, once he walked up to her and got her attention.

"Hey, boo! Let me finishing with him, and I definitely got you," Strawberry told the sexy guy.

But Strawberry quickly lost interest in the man for whom she was dancing, when she saw Boss pull out a phat knot of cash.

"You got time for me now, shorty?" Boss asked, seeing the look on her face when she stared at the money he pulled out.

"Hold up!" the man who Strawberry had been dancing for spoke up as Strawberry began to leave him before he grabbed her arm. "Fuck this nigga! His money ain't no better than my shit!"

"Yeah! But I see twenties and even fifties, while you're throwing a bitch ones, nigga! Let me go!" Strawberry told the guy, pulling away from him and turning to face Mr. Sexy. "What's up, boo? Where you wanna go? We can get a room in the back if that's what you want."

"Boss!"

Hearing his name before he could respond to Strawberry, Boss looked back behind him and paused for a moment, instantly recognizing that he was looking at Vanity.

Vanity broke out a smile and rushed over to Boss. She threw her arms around his neck, hugged him, and held him a moment, feeling his arms around her.

"What are you doing here, Boss?" she said as she pulled back to meet his eyes.

"Ummm! I'm with a friend," Boss answered, nodding over to Eazy.

He then looked her over in her black thong and bra and asked, "You work here?"

"Yes!" she answered, taking Boss's hand and leading him out of the VIP section.

Strawberry caught up to them and grabbed Boss's arm as she pulled him and tried to get him away from Vanity.

"He's with me, Pleasure!" Strawberry told her with an attitude, not about to let Mr. Sexy leave after seeing his bank roll.

"Strawberry, this is my boyfriend!" Vanity lied, pulling Boss back in her direction.

"Well he came looking for me!" Strawberry replied.

"Whoa!" Boss spoke up before he called over to Eazy, who was standing a few feet away with a grin.

"Take care of my buddy, and I got you, shorty," Boss told Strawberry as he nodded over at Eazy.

Strawberry sucked her teeth and shot Vanity a look before grabbing Mr. Sexy's friend and leading him off. Strawberry brushed past Vanity and mumbled. Vanity shook her head and locked back on to Boss.

"Is that what I have to always deal with when I'm with you?"

Boss shrugged his shoulders and smirked, allowing a smiling Vanity to grab his hand again and lead him away from the VIP area.

# SEVEN

**"SO, THIS WHERE YOU** work, huh?" Boss asked Vanity once the two of them were inside a dimly lit room that had only a black leather sofa and a black round wood table.

Vanity smiled as she sat beside Boss and just looked at him. She remembered the fact that she didn't hear from him, and before she knew it, she punched him in the arm. "Why haven't you called me yet?"

Boss rubbed his arm and looked at her like she was crazy. "I'm not really into breaking up happy homes, shorty."

"What are you talking about?"

"Dude at the bus station. Malcolm!"

"Boss, I told you about Malcolm, and I also told you that wasn't serious."

"So, from what you're saying, you and this Malcolm dude are just buddies, right?"

"That's exactly what I'm saying!"

"So you tongue kiss all your buddies, huh?"

Vanity was caught off guard. She stared at Boss and remembered the way Malcolm had greeted her at the bus station in front of Boss. She never got the chance to defend herself, as Boss changed the subject.

"So, how long you been working here?"

"A little over four years ago now!" Vanity answered him. "How do you know Eazy?"

"We ran into each other and just connected," Boss answered. "So, what time you getting off?"

"About four thirty, why?"

"You wanna get something to eat after work? We can chill and talk."

"Chill and talk, huh?" Vanity asked, smiling at him. "Alright, Boss! Meet me here at 4:00 p.m., and we can get something to eat."

Boss dug out his bankroll and handed her $300, as he got up off the sofa.

"Do me a favor. Find out where your girl Strawberry took Eazy and tell 'im to come holla at me."

"Okay!" Vanity answered, holding up the money he gave her. "What's this for?"

"Your time!"

"I give you my time for free, Boss," Vanity said, handing him back his money.

Boss then watched as Vanity carried her sexy-as-hell frame out of the room. He couldn't help shake his head as he sat back down on the sofa to wait.

* * *

Boss looked up from his phone a few minutes after texting a reply to Brandi. He then heard the room door open and first saw Strawberry walk inside followed by Eazy, who was shaking his head and smirking.

"Tired of Pleasure's ass, huh?" Strawberry asked, smiling as she walked straight up to Boss and sat on his lap. "So, what's up, boo? What you want?"

"Help!!" Boss answered before he continued. "I'ma give you five stacks if you help me find your brother."

"You mean Cash?" she asked him. "What you want with him?"

"He owes me a lot of money, and I want to collect."

"What are you gonna do to him? Are you going to beat him

up?"

"If he doesn't have my money, then pretty much!" Boss lied. "You helping me or what?"

"You're not gonna kill him, are you?" she asked, wanting the money but not wanting to see her brother dead.

"I can't get paid if he's dead, shorty," Boss told her.

Strawberry then nodded her head in agreement to what Boss had just said. "Okay. I'ma help you," she answered, holding out her hand for the money that was promised to her.

\* \* \*

Back inside the locker room, after Mr. Sexy and his friend left the club, Strawberry got out her cell phone from her gym bag and called her brother's phone number.

"Yeah!"

"Cash, this is Pam. Where you at?"

"What's up, Pam?"

"Where you at?"

"Handling some business. Why?"

"Because I need you to come up to the club. It's these three white guys out here, and I just went through it with one of them. He put his hands on me because I wouldn't give his lil'-dick ass no dance!"

"They still there now?"

"Yeah!"

"Alright. I'm on my way."

After hanging up the phone with her brother, Pam then called the phone number given to her by Boss.

"Yo!"

"Hey, boo! This Strawberry."

"What's up, sexy?"

"I did as you wanted. Cash is on his way to the club now."

"Good girl!"

"So, when can I see you again?"

"Tell you what. What time you get off work tonight?"

"I'm supposed to leave at four thirty, but for you I'll leave whenever you want me to!"

"I'ma hit you back at this number, and then we can hook up, alright?"

"How long, boo?"

"Be by the phone in two hours."

"I will definitely be waiting."

After hanging up the phone with Mr. Sexy, Strawberry smiled at the thought of all the money she was about to get out of his fine but stupid ass. Pam actually could feel her pussy getting wet at the thought of all the money Boss had pulled out and shown her.

\* \* \*

.

Boss waited inside the strip club's parking lot after hanging up with Strawberry. He told Eazy what she had told him. Boss then sat blowing a blunt with Eazy and discussing what both of them agreed was now a partnership.

"What's up with this dude you was telling me about who's your pill connect?" Boss asked. "We gonna need more roxies after what we get finished."

"You talking about my nigga Rico?" Eazy stated. "I'ma get at 'im about that and see if we can meet up and holla at him."

"That'll work!" Boss replied. "I'ma get at my dude back in Atlanta who was fucking with me on the coke business. I'ma connect back up with him since his shit is good."

"How you feel about bringing in a third person?" Eazy asked Boss as he passed the blunt back.

"You talking about your boy Rico?" Boss asked, looking over at Eazy.

"He's solid, my nigga," Eazy stated. "I've been fucking with him for years, and my nigga's good people, Boss. Trust me."

Boss nodded his head slowly and then looked back at Eazy and said, "Alright! But you're responsible for your man if shit turns out bad."

"I'm on it!" Eazy replied with a smile.

Boss remained quiet for a brief moment while watching the entrance to the parking lot.

"How are Mom and Pops? They good after the shit that happened at the Pit?" Boss asked, breaking the silence.

"They good!" Eazy answered. "Erica called and told me they followed my mom and father home and chilled with them a little while."

"Why don't your mom and pops just open up a restaurant instead of being out on the street?" Boss asked him. "It's easy to see that they'll be crazy busy once they open up a restaurant."

"Yeah, they do good business, but they ain't been doing it long and they really ain't got the money yet to open a permanent place," Eazy explained. "They've talked about it, but there's a lot of shit that comes with opening up a restaurant."

"How much do they need?" Boss asked him.

"I remember my father saying they spoke with some people and the number was about $35,000–$40,000."

Boss nodded his head and started asking another question, when he spotted the familiar-looking Impala SS that turned into the parking lot.

"Ain't that your boy there?" Boss said as he nodded toward the car.

Eazy recognized the Impala and began climbing out of the Porsche at the same time Boss did. The pair calmly started across the parking lot just as Cash was climbing out of the driver's seat and Grip was climbing out from the passenger's side.

"Muthafucker! What's up?" Boss said in a voice just above a whisper at the same time he placed the barrel of his .45 up against Cash's back.

"Bitch ass!"

"You was saying something, nigga?" Eazy interrupted as he dropped his forearm up against Grip's neck and pressed his 9mm into the side of his head after sliding up on him.

Boss shifted his eyes back toward Cash.

"This is how this shit's going: You niggas are coming with us, and we'll finish that conversation we was having back at the Pit," Boss said.

* * *

Vanity tried to control herself as she tried to get through the rest of the night, but she was having a hard time focusing with thoughts of ReSean "Boss" Holmes on her mind from twenty minutes ago. She was dancing with a customer when another one of the dancers came up to her to let her know that she had a VIP request. Vanity finished up her lap dance with the guy she was dancing with, gave him a kiss on the cheek, and then rushed off to the locker room to get cleaned up.

Five minutes later, Vanity changed into a pink G-string and bra set, left the locker room, and started walking toward the stairs that led to the VIP area. As she passed Strawberry, she caught the look she gave her, but Vanity ignored it and continued up the steps. There she saw Malcolm and his best friend and partner waiting inside the VIP section for her.

"What's up, Vanity?" Moses spoke up as he was walking past her and leaving the VIP section.

Vanity walked toward Malcolm after Moses walked downstairs.

"What are you doing here?" Vanity asked as Malcolm gave her a cute smile.

"I missed you!" Malcolm told her as he pulled her onto his lap and then wrapped his arms around her. "I wanted to see you, so I'm here. That's cool with you, right?"

"That's fine, Malcolm," Vanity told him, smiling as she loosely wrapped her arms around his neck, only for him to lean in and kiss her directly on the lips.

"Malcolm, slowly, please!" she said as she pulled out of the kiss.

"Vanity, come on!" Malcolm said with a sigh. "We've been doing this for six months and you're still pushing me away. What's up? If you're not interested, then just tell me."

"Malcolm, you know I'm attracted to you, but I'm just not ready yet," Vanity told him gently stroking the side of his face.

"Alright! How about I come by after you get off and we relax at your place or mine?" Malcolm sighed.

"Can we re-schedule?"

"Why?"

"I've got plans, Malcolm."

"With whom?"

"A friend, Malcolm."

"What friend?"

"Malcolm, look," Vanity began, trying to keep her calm, "I've got plans, and if you want to go out tomorrow night since it's Sunday and the club is closed, we can do something then."

"Whatever!" Malcolm replied with a light pat to Vanity's ass for her to get up from his lap.

"Oh, so you leaving now?" Vanity asked as she stood up from his lap and saw that he was upset.

"I got business to handle," Malcolm replied as he started for the stairs, leaving Vanity watching him, shaking her head.

* * *

Boss waited in the parking lot at Pink Palace after dealing with both Cash and Grip and dropping Eazy back at this ride at the hotel. He sat smoking a blunt, when his cell phone went off. When he picked it up, he saw Brandi was calling.

"What's up, shorty?" he answered the phone.

"Where you at, ReSean?"

"Waiting to handle one last thing!"

"So I guess I'll see you tonight then, huh?"

"Why? You miss me, shorty?"

"ReSean, look! All jokes aside, I'm really interested in getting to know you, and I want us to try being in a relationship. But if you're not really interested, let me know and I'll move on."

"You finished? "

"ReSean, I'm serious!"

"I know," he told her. "I also know that I was very clear

when I said that I was into getting to—"

Boss paused when he recognized the guy who walked out of the club with a muscular-built dude at his side. Boss sat staring at the same Malcolm who was at the Greyhound station to pick up Vanity, and now he was at the Pink Palace where she worked.

"ReSean!" Brandi yelled into the phone.

"Yeah!" Boss answered as he continued watching Malcolm walk over to his Mercedes SLG3 AMG.

"Baby! What's wrong? Are you okay?" Brandi asked, sounding worried.

"Yeah, I'm good!" Boss answered as he continued watching as the Benz drove out of the parking lot.

He then looked back to the club just as Strawberry was walking outside.

"Text me your address and I'll be there in a little while," Boss told Brandi before he hung up.

When Strawberry walked up to the passenger side door of Boss's Porsche, he hit the locks. After she opened the car door and climbed inside, Boss started the engine.

"Hey, boo!" Pam said, smiling as she leaned over and kissed Boss's cheek. "Sorry it took me so long. I had to talk to the owner before he let me leave."

"It's cool!" Boss replied as he was leaving the club's parking lot.

"Boo, what's wrong? You okay?" Pam asked when she saw Boss's facial expression and heard the flat tone in his voice.

"Just something on my mind."

"You wanna talk about it?"

"Malcolm. You know him?" Boss asked after a brief moment.

"You mean Malcolm White?" Pam asked him. "Everybody knows who he is. Why?"

"I saw him leaving the club just now. What's he doing here?"

"You must not like him!" Pam said. "Pleasure is Malcolm's girlfriend. They've been seeing each other almost a year now."

"So, they're dating, huh?"

"Of course!" Pam answered. "You don't half-step with Malcolm White. He's just like his father used to be before Malcolm White Sr. retired and left everything to his son."

"And how do you know all of this?" Boss asked as he glanced over at Strawberry.

"I used to deal with Malcolm for a little while until he started fucking Pleasure's ass," Pam explained with a little roll of the eyes.

Pam smiled as she leaned over to Boss. She reached over between his legs and began caressing his dick. "There's a hotel close by. We can go there tonight."

"Direct the way!" Boss told her as she unzipped and opened his jeans.

He glanced down as she pulled out his semi-hard dick, slid her mouth down it, and began to suck him deeply.

\* \* \*

Boss arrived at the hotel to which Strawberry had directed him. He gave her money to rent a room, and then he parked his Porsche by the exit. After a few minutes, he entered the hotel and saw Strawberry flirting with a white boy behind the front desk, but she said goodbye when she saw Boss enter the lobby.

"We're on the second floor in room 21," Pam told Boss,

grabbing his hand and leading him toward the elevator.

They rode the elevator, and Boss allowed Strawberry to lead him to their room. Once they stepped inside and locked the door behind them, Boss walked over to the bed.

"Come here!" Pam told him.

She walked up on Boss and reached straight for his jeans, undid them, and let down the zipper. She saw him remove a chrome gun from his back and then sit down on the bed.

"Let me finish what I started inside the car, boo!"

"Handle your business, shorty!" Boss told her, watching as she kicked off her shoes and then undressed down to her panties and bra.

Boss held her eyes as she lowered herself to her knees and, within moments, had his dick deep inside her throat. She was going to work and making love to his shit.

Boss watched Strawberry as she put in the work, and he admitted to himself that she had some skills. Boss ignored all the dick sucking as he grabbed the pillow from the head of the bed. Before Strawberry could figure out what was about to happen, Boss lowered the pillow to her head and then quickly placed his .45 against it.

*Boom!*

Boss saw blood and brains fly out from under the pillow after blowing out Strawberry's brains, killing her since both her brother and Grip were both bodied because of her. Boss didn't even bother watching the body drop. He was already fixing his clothes and then stepped over her body and headed for the room door to exit.

Boss headed down the elevator and walked into the lobby. Just as he was about to walk out the front doors, he thought about the hotel clerk. When Boss turned around to look at him, the clerk was on the phone laughing. Boss walked over to him and got his attention. He calmly walked behind the front desk and silenced the young man by pointing his .45 in his face.

"Hang up the phone."

Doing as he was told, the clerk stared up at the gun in front of him, unable to say anything.

"Where's the camera at?" Boss asked the guy in a lowered voice.

"In-in the back office!" the clerk got out, stumbling over his words.

"Back office only?"

"Yes!"

*Boom! Boom!*

Boss watched as the clerk's face disappeared before his body flew back out of the desk chair he sat on. Boss then turned and entered the office to look for the camera recordings.

# EIGHT

**BOSS WOKE UP TO** the sound of a ringing phone and Brandi gently pushing against his side and moaning his name. He slowly opened his eyes and first looked down at Brandi lying on his chest. He then looked over to where he had set his phone and banger on top of the bedside table. He reached over and picked up the phone, glanced at the screen, and answered.

"Yeah?"

"Boss, what's up, my nigga? You asleep?"

"Naw. What's up though?"

"Bruh, I gotta holla at you about something, and also I got at my nigga Rico. He's ready to meet up and talk business."

"Alright. Listen, we'll meet up, but it's gonna have to be quick, because I got some stuff I wanna handle today."

"Where at?"

Boss remained quiet for a moment as he remembered a spot he saw the day before after the Strawberry issue.

"We'll meet right there at that building inside the parking lot at the 183rd Street flea market off of 27th Avenue. Also, I'ma need you to call your mom and have her call me. Let her know that I really need to talk to her about something important."

"I got you, my nigga."

After hanging up with Eazy, Boss noticed that he had missed four calls, all of which were from Vanity.

"What exactly do you have planned today?" Brandi said to Boss as she lifted her head from his chest, only to rest her chin on his chest and meet his eyes.

"I got a few things I wanna do," he told her, gently brushing her hair out of her face.

"What exactly is that?" she asked as she began tracing her finger along the tattoo on the left side of Boss's chest.

His tattoo was a picture of Jesus's hands together in prayer holding a Cuban-link chain with a cross charm hanging from the chain with the words Son of God beneath the hands and chain.

"You'll find out when we get there!" Boss told her, just as Brandi's phone began ringing from the other bedside table on the far right side of the bed.

Boss climbed out of the bed once Brandi rolled over to answer her phone. He then headed into the bathroom. He didn't worry about closing the door behind him, so he went ahead and handled his business on the toilet.

Once he was done and had washed his hands, Boss stripped naked and climbed into the shower. Just as he was turning on the shower water and standing beneath the shower head, the shower curtain was pulled back, and Brandi got in with him.

"You got a phone call!" Brandi told Boss, holding the phone out and away from the water so it wouldn't get wet.

Boss took the phone, stepped out from under the water, and caught the mischievous look that Brandi was giving him as he held the phone up to his ear.

"Yeah!"

"Hi, ReSean, sweety. You wanted to speak with me about something?" Evelyn Collins asked once she heard Boss's voice over the line.

"Yes, ma'am," Boss answered, looking at Brandi as she wrapped her hand around his dick and smirked. "I spoke with Erick last night and wanted to make sure you and Mr. Collins made it home safely, but then I questioned him about the reason you two don't have an indoor restaurant. Everybody loves the food the two of you cook."

"ReSean, we're working toward that same goal now!" Evelyn told Boss. "After last night though, Darrell and I both decided we need to find a new location."

"Mrs. Collins, can you do me a favor, please?"

"What is it, honey?"

"Can you and Mr. Collins meet me on 183rd Street and 27th Avenue inside the parking lot of the flea market? There's a building I want you to see."

"ReSean, we don't have—!"

"Mrs. Collins, please!" Boss told her, cutting her off. "Just humor me."

Evelyn sighed through the phone, gave in, and said, "Okay, ReSean! When are we meeting there?"

Boss told Mrs. Collins what time to be at the location and then hung up the phone. He then focused his attention back to Brandi. who had been gently and slowly stroking his dick the whole time he was on the phone. But she was now smiling up at him.

"You plan on taking care of that now that you got him up, shorty?" Boss questioned.

"I will, depending on how you answer my question," Brandi told him, adding a little more pressure while stroking Boss's manhood.

"And exactly what question is that?" Boss asked, reaching up to touch Brandi's nipple, only to have her pull away and shake her head no at him.

"Don't touch!" she told him with a smile. "When are you going to answer my question about us? Are we going to try us or not, ReSean?"

"You sure you're ready to fuck with a dude like me,

shorty?"

"I'll admit that you're the youngest guy I've ever wanted to be with, but I'm sure I want to see how things can be between us. You know already it's been two years since I've been with anyone, so you know there are no games being played, ReSean! What are you going to do?"

Boss slowly nodded his head while holding Brandi's hazel-colored eyes. Finally he said, "Take care of your man, shorty! You got me up, so now relax me!"

"Anything my man wants!" Brandi responded with a smile as she slowly lowered herself to her knees in front of Boss.

She first kissed the head of his dick before taking only the head into her mouth, all while looking up into his eyes as he stared down at her.

* * *

Brandi wanted to do more than suck her man's dick and let him lick her pussy, but she understood that he had business to take care of. She was happy with what they shared and was now dressed in a Dolce & Gabbana outfit and seated inside the passenger seat of Boss's Porsche as he drove to the hotel he told her he was staying at until he found a place to live.

Once at his hotel, Brandi only had to wait eight minutes until Boss was dressed in a black and cream-colored Gucci outfit, along with a black and white Yankees fitted cap. She was on the phone talking with Maxine when he walked up behind her fully dressed and carrying a backpack.

"You ready?" Boss asked, after kissing her on the neck.

Brandi smiled at the feel of his lips on her neck. She then turned and kissed him on the lips, and they started toward the room door.

"So, are you planning on telling me what's going on?" Brandi asked as they rode the elevator down to the lobby.

"What about?" Boss asked.

"What's up with having Eazy and his parents meet you at some building at 183rd Street?"

Boss remained silent as they stepped off the elevator and crossed through the lobby. He didn't speak again until he and Brandi were back inside the Porsche.

"I'm meeting Eazy and one of his boys at the flea market on some business-type shit. But I'm meeting Mr. and Mrs. Collins there as well, because of a business offer I want to run by them."

"It's not my business, but what type of business proposal are you offering Mr. and Mrs. Collins, ReSean?"

"Opening a soul food and barbecue restaurant," Boss said to Brandi as he glanced from the road over to her.

Boss saw a huge smile spread across Brandi's face as she understood what he had just told her, though she really didn't know the entire story. Boss drove smiling and thinking about how things would turn out if the Collinses accepted his offer.

* * *

Eazy saw Boss's Porsche as it pulled up to the entrance of the building that was for lease. Eazy nodded to the Porsche, letting Rico know Boss was there, and both he and Rico climbed from the Lexus as Boss was turning into the parking lot.

"This dude is pushing a Porsche?" Rico asked in a thick Spanish accent as he and Eazy started toward the Porsche Twin

Turbo.

"Let's just say my nigga is about his issues!" Eazy replied as Boss was climbing from the car, only to see somebody reach across the seat and hand him something.

"What's good, fellas?" Boss said as Eazy and a light-skinned Spanish man walked up.

Rico had a little size around the middle, but he also had a good upper body.

Eazy embraced Boss and then introduced the men to one another.

"What's good, playboy?" Boss asked, dapping up with Rico.

"What's up?" Rico replied, but then said, "You look kind of young."

"Does my being younger matter as long as we get money?" Boss asked Rico.

"I feel that!" Rico replied, nodding his head in understanding.

"Now that we got that out of the way, Eazy was telling me that you got the connect for the pills."

"Whatever you want!" Rico said, smiling.

"I'ma need you to set up a meeting with me and your connect to have a sit-down so we can discuss a deal on pills."

"What type of pills you trying to get?" Rico asked him.

"Roxies!" Eazy answered as he heard the car door open and watched Brandi climb out.

"ReSean, your phone's ringing!" Brandi told him, walking around the back end of the car and handing Boss his cell phone.

"Yeah!" Boss replied once he saw it was Vanity on his phone.

"Hi! What happened last night?"

"I got caught up handling something, but I'm pretty sure you had a back plan since the nigga Malcolm came back to the spot after I left."

"Who told you that?"

"It don't even matter," Boss told her. "Listen though, I'm in the middle of something right now. We'll finish this later."

Boss hung up the phone before Vanity could say anything else. Boss then handed the phone back to a hard-staring Brandi.

"We'll talk about that phone call later!" Brandi said to Boss.

Boss watched as Brandi walked off back around the car. He shook his head and looked back at Eazy and Rico.

"I don't know how you got something that sexy, but I'm with whatever you're doing, my nigga!" Rico called out.

Boss continued discussing business plans with Eazy and Rico until he saw the white and maroon Lincoln Town Car turn into the parking lot. Boss quickly spotted Evelyn Collins inside the passenger seat as it drove past.

"We'll finish this discussion later," Boss told Rick and Eazy as Evelyn and Darrell climbed from the car.

"Hey, Momma!" Eazy yelled, happy at seeing his mother. He walked over to Evelyn and hugged her and kissed her on the cheek.

"Hey, sweety!" Evelyn replied, smiling at her son as she wrapped her arms around his waist. She then looked at Boss and said, "Okay, ReSean! We're here. So, what's so important?"

"What's going on?" Eazy asked, looking from his mother over to Boss and then to his father and back to Boss.

"Hold on!" Boss said, turning back to the car and opening the car door.

"You finished?" Brandi asked with a slight attitude.

"Naw!" Boss answered as he picked up his phone. "Mrs. Collins is out here." Climbing back out of the car, Boss pulled up the number of the person he was waiting on. As he made his call, he followed Brandi with his eyes as she walked over to her godmother.

"Hello!" the male voice said over the line once the phone was answered.

Boss questioned the man on the other end asking him where he was and how long it would take for his arrival. Boss then hung up the phone and walked back over to join the others.

"Are you ready to tell us what's going on, ReSean?" Evelyn asked Boss as he stopped beside Eazy.

"I have someone coming here to meet with you and Mr. Collins about that building," Boss told the couple. "If you remember our conversation earlier, I asked about you and Mr. Collins opening a restaurant. You remember?"

"Of course, ReSean!" Evelyn answered. "I told my husband you and I spoke."

Boss looked at Mr. Collins and said, "Mr. Collins, sir. I understand you and Mrs. Collins only just met me, but I have an offer I would like to run past you two."

"We're listening," Darrell Collins replied, just as a royal-blue Chrysler 300 pulled up to the parking lot and turned in.

Boss watched the car park and then excused himself from the others and walked over to greet the driver.

"What in God's name is this child up to?" Evelyn asked, watching Boss speaking and shaking hands with a dark-haired white man in a blue suit and glasses.

"Boss has an offer he wants to talk to you and daddy about," Brandi told Evelyn, smiling at her godmother.

"You know what this is all about, don't you, Brandi?" Evelyn asked as both Boss and the white man walked over to join them.

"Mr. and Mrs. Collins, this is Antonio Wells, and he is the agent responsible for leasing this building to its new owners."

"New owners?" Evelyn repeated with a confused expression on her face.

She then looked to her husband, who stood staring straight at Boss.

"Ma'am. Sir. Would you like to look at the building now?" Mr. Wells asked as he started toward the building.

"ReSean, what is going on?" Evelyn asked, grabbing his arm and pulling him over to her.

"I'm giving you and Mr. Collins the money you need to open your restaurant. The only thing I ask is to be a silent partner. Both you and Mr. Collins will have full say so on what happens. I will only be a part of the business silently. What do you say?"

"ReSean, are you serious?" Evelyn asked in disbelief at what she was hearing. "Where did you possibly get enough money to do this?"

"I saved it!" Boss told her before walking back to the Porsche.

"He's serious, isn't he?" Evelyn asked, looking first at her husband and then at Brandi and a smiling Eazy.

"We ready?" Boss asked as he walked back over carrying his backpack.

* * *

Boss wanted to get a first look at the building that was

originally a restaurant but had been closed for business for a while. Boss allowed Antonio Wells to show Mr. and Mrs. Collins the building that was a lot larger than it actually looked from the outside.

Once the tour was finished, he looked at both Mr. and Mrs. Collins and asked, "So, what's it going to be? Do we have a deal?"

"You're really serious about this, son?" Darrell asked.

"Take a look, sir," Boss said as he handed Mr. Collins his backpack.

Darrell opened the backpack and looked inside at all the money. He then looked back at Boss with a shocked look on his face.

"Oh my God!" Evelyn cried in shock from the sight of all the money inside the backpack.

"ReSean, where'd you get all this money?"

"I saved it!" Boss told her. "There's $40,000 inside there. That should be enough to start things up; but if more is needed, let me know. So, do we have a deal?"

Darrell slowly nodded his head and then looked over at his wife and the look she was giving him.

"You've got a deal, son!" Darrell said as he turned back toward Boss and held out his hand.

# NINE

**VANITY WAITED AROUND HER** condo for Boss to call her back, trying to ignore the fact that over five hours had passed since he said he would call her back earlier. Vanity ignored Malcolm and her girlfriends' calls, and she was beginning to get very upset that he still had not called her back.

"Forget this!" Vanity said out loud, picking up her phone from the coffee table.

She pulled up Boss's phone number and called him.

"Yeah!" Boss answered at the start of the third ring.

"Boss! Where are you?" Vanity asked as she stood up from her sofa, with her right hand holding the phone to her ear while her left hand was on her hip.

"At the moment I'm doing some shopping for my new apartment. What's up though?"

"What's up?" Vanity repeated. "Boss, why do I feel like you're ignoring me? If you've lost interest, then just tell me. Don't have me chasing you and playing the fool!"

"Playing the fool you say, huh?" Boss repeated, before telling Vanity to hold on.

Vanity was surprised by Boss's attitude. She was trying to understand what had happened between the two of them, when Boss came back over the line.

"Vanity!"

"I'm here, Boss!"

"Listen, shorty! We're not gonna play games with each other. I'm going to say this one last time because I'm not sure if you understood me last time. Yeah, I'm feeling you and would have wanted to kick it with you to see where things could have went between us, but I'm not into beefing with a nigga about his lady, because my beef ends the same way, and it ain't with me getting fucked up."

"Boss, what are you talking about?"

"I'm talking about that nigga Malcolm and the type of relationship you two got going on!"

"Boss, I've already told you!"

"I know what you told me!" Boss began, cutting her off. "But I also see how you two react to each other! What type of friend kisses the way you two do, and the way homeboy reacts to you shows that it's something more; and I'd really hate to get into it with that dude Malcolm about his girl."

"Boss, I'm not his girl!"

"How do I know that?"

"Because I'm telling you I'm not!"

"Just like you told me Malcolm came to the club last night or that you two are supposedly friends for almost a year now, huh?" Boss asked. "Vanity, look! I'm feeling you no doubt, but I really ain't trying to fuck a nigga up about you when you're not even my woman. So get at me when you're free, ma!"

After Boss hung up, Vanity stared at her phone for a few minutes, repeating in her head what Boss had just told her. She then pulled up another number and called the one person she knew was about to really act a fool.

"Yeah!" Malcolm answered at the start of the second ring.

\* \* \*

Boss walked back into the Bed, Bath & Beyond store after hanging up with Vanity. He found Brandi looking at a bed set and talking with a female salesperson. He then walked up beside Brandi and wrapped his arms around her waist only to have her shrug him away.

"Do you like this or not?" Brandi asked Boss sharply, shooting him a look.

"Yeah! It's cool!" Boss answered.

He then grabbed for Brandi's hand to pull her off to the side, only to have her pull away from him and walk off with the saleswoman. Boss shook his head, knowing what was wrong with her. He decided to just leave her alone for a few minutes, so he turned and headed for the exit. He then remembered seeing a Best Buy up the street from the Bed, Bath & Beyond.

Boss left the store and decided to walk the few blocks to Best Buy. He reached the store and was just entering when his phone rang inside the case in his hip.

"What's good, playboy?" Boss answered, after seeing Eazy was calling on his iPhone.

"Boss, where you at, my nigga?"

"At Best Buy. Why?"

"Bruh, I gotta holla at you about something. Tell me which Best Buy you're at."

After giving Eazy the location of the Best Buy in Hollywood, Boss hung up the phone and turned his attention to the 38" plasma flat-screen television. Boss continued walking around and ended up in the game section looking at a PlayStation 4 and an Xbox.

"Do you need any help, sir?" a red-headed female employee inquired as she walked up to Boss on his left side.

"I pretty much do!" Boss answered, looking back at the game system.

* * *

Boss finished picking out what he wanted and arranged to have everything delivered to the new house he was renting. Boss was just stepping back outside of the store when he saw Eazy's Lexus swing into the Best Buy parking lot.

Boss walked out into the middle of the parking lot as Eazy was pulling up his Lexus. Boss walked around to the passenger side, just as Rico was climbing out of the front seat and getting into the back. He then took Rico's place up front beside Eazy.

"What's good, fellas?" Boss asked once he was inside the car.

"What's up, my nigga?" Eazy said as he was pulling off. "Bruh, they found Strawberry's body as well as the hotel clerk at the Best Western. Also, what I just heard is that this nigga Victor White just put a $30,000 reward out on the niggas involved in Lucky's murder. But then you got this nigga Berry with different niggas calling me to look for your ass. He's done had ten different niggas calling me for him about some more blue devils. We may as well open up shop that way!"

"Turn up in here!" Boss told Eazy, nodding toward the entrance to Bed, Bath, & Beyond.

"Where's this nigga Victor White at?"

"I hear he's at the Hilton out in South Beach, but the nigga has a team with his ass!" Eazy told Boss.

"Find out this nigga's room and where he moves to," Boss told Eazy.

He then called back to Rico.

"I want you to set up shop over in Berry's area around the M&M store. I'ma get at Berry and let him know to bring the customers to you, but I want you to look out for the nigga Berry! He don't pay, but don't give his ass too much. I don't want the nigga riding on our ass. And as far as Strawberry, let shorty rest in peace!"

Boss reached for his phone when it began ringing. He pulled out his iPhone and saw Brandi was calling him. He then motioned to both Eazy and Rico to hold on.

"Yeah. What's up, Brandi?"

"ReSean, where are you? I've paid for some of this stuff for the house, but I didn't bring a lot of money with me. Can you come and pay for the rest?"

"I'ma be inside in a few minutes," Boss told her, hanging up the phone and looking back toward Eazy.

"I'm glad you two are here. I'ma need some help fixing up my spot and getting everything put together."

Boss told Eazy and Rico to wait for him. He then got out of the Lexus and walked back inside the store and saw Brandi heading his way.

"Where'd you go?" she asked, once she and Boss met up.

"I went down the street to Best Buy," Boss told her, following Brandi through the store.

"Why didn't you let me go with you?" Brandi asked, looking over at Boss with a look on her face.

Boss didn't get the chance to answer Brandi's question as the two of them met up with the same female salesperson and Boss paid the rest of the bill.

"Eazy and Rico are outside waiting. They're helping with moving the stuff inside the house. But then I gotta handle something," Boss informed Brandi.

"We need to talk also," Brandi told him, rolling her eyes at Boss.

* * *

Boss left Bed, Bath & Beyond with Eazy following behind them as they drove over to the gated community in Hollywood Oaks. They drove through the front gate using a passcode to Boss's new three-bedroom house. After turning into the driveway and parking in front of the two-car garage, Eazy parked beside Boss's car. Boss then shut off the car and then both he and Brandi climbed out of his Porsche.

"So, this is where you're at, bruh?" Eazy asked as he climbed out of his ride and looked around.

"This is it for the moment!" Boss answered as he followed Brandi to the front door.

Once Brandi used the key Boss had given her, Boss, Eazy, and Rico followed her inside the house.

"Erica, Maxine, and two more of my girls are coming over to help me set things up, ReSean!" Brandi told Boss. "Let me talk to you before you entertain your boys, please."

Boss watched as Brandi walked off and headed toward the back of the house. Boss shook his head and then told Eazy and Rico to chill until he returned. He then followed behind Brandi, where he found her sitting in the master bedroom.

"ReSean, what's going on?" Brandi asked as soon as Boss entered the bedroom. "What's going on with you and Vanity?"

"So you actually do know shorty, huh?" Boss asked with a smirk. "When was you planning to tell me you danced at the Pink Palace, ma?"

"Does it matter?"

"Does my knowing Vanity matter?"

"Yes the hell it does!" Brandi stated with an attitude. "I don't share my nigga with no bitch, ReSean! I know who the fuck Vanity is, and I don't like that bitch, and I don't want my man around that bitch. Period!"

"You finished?" Boss calmly asked, but started back up before she could answer. "First, understand that I'm your man, not your child. I'll respect you, but you don't decide who I'm around or who I'm friends with! Whatever issue you and Vanity got going on needs to stop! Your only concern is us!"

"As long as you remember that's exactly what we are—us—I won't cut up; but the first time that bitch gets out of the line, ReSean, I will act a fool! Are we clear on that?" Brandi demanded, stepping up on Boss and staring him directly in his eyes.

Boss slowly shook his head but smirked down at Brandi. He then gripped her by the waist and pulled her up against him as he bent his head and kissed her lips while gripping her ass in both hands. Brandi was just wrapping her arms up and around his neck when knocking started at the bedroom door, right before Maxine called out for Brandi from the other side of the door.

"Sorry!" Brandi told Boss, smiling as she released him and then pulled away and started toward the door.

She opened to door to see Maxine, Erica, Regina, and Tina crowded together and blocking the doorway.

"Where's he at, Brandi?" Regina asked, looking past her girl to get a better look inside the bedroom.

Brandi was sucking her teeth and about to tell her girls that she would see them in the living room, when she felt Boss's hard muscular body press up against hers. She smelled his cologne and instantly lay back against him.

"What's up, ladies?" Boss said, in his smooth, mildly deep voice.

"Damn!" Tina cried, seeing Boss for the first time.

"Girl, his ass is fine!" Regina added.

Boss smiled as he bent down and kissed Brandi's cheek and then her lips as she lifted her head for a kiss. Boss told her he was heading back into the living room with Eazy and Rico.

As Brandi watched her man walk out of the bedroom, she also noticed all her girls do the same. She shook her head and interrupted her girls as she playfully pushed through the middle of them.

"You hookers stop staring at my man and come on! We need to get ready for when the furniture arrives."

\* \* \*

Boss showed his boys around the new house, and then they chilled outside on the back patio smoking until the furniture arrived. Boss and the guys got to work helping the girls with setting up things where they wanted everything to go. Boss took care of the den himself, setting up his game room with his PlayStation 4 and flat-screen television. He also set up his Xbox in one of the bedrooms.

Boss, Eazy, and Rico did most of what the other girls asked them to do, until Eazy received another call from another person from Berry. Boss then told Brandi that he had to leave to handle some business. He kissed her goodbye, leaving his car keys with her, before he, Eazy, and Rico headed out the front door.

"Slide by the hotel real quick," Boss told Eazy, once inside the Lexus. "I wanna pick up the rest of the blue devils and grab the other shit, too."

"I was gonna holla at you earlier, also," Eazy told Boss. "Rico got at me about this spot out in Opa-locka that's open for work. It's a house owned by this smoker bitch whose old man got locked up about two years ago. It's a good spot directly in the hood, but the only problem is that there's this nigga named Brandon Cook and his team that's supposedly running the area. What you wanna do?"

"You say it's in the middle of the hood, huh?" Boss asked him.

"Yeah!" Rico answered. "The nigga king had the area on smash until somebody put the police on the man."

Boss nodded his head and remained quiet for a moment.

"Alright, let's take care of this shit with Berry, and then we'll go see what's up with this spot out there in Opa-locka!" Boss continued.

\* \* \*

Vanity stepped out the front door of her apartment and locked it behind her. She started toward the exit of the complex, walking through the hallway. Just as she was stepping into the parking lot, she saw Malcolm climb out of his Mercedes.

"Here we go!" she said to herself with a sigh, seeing the look on his face.

"Vanity!" Malcolm called out as she continued walking.

He knew she saw him when she slowed up.

"Vanity, hold up!"

Vanity heard Malcolm, but she ignored his call as she walked over to her Corvette Stingray convertible. She was unlocking the driver's door when Malcolm walked up and pushed the car door shut as she was opening it.

"So, is this how it is now, huh?" Malcolm asked Vanity. "You ignoring me now, right?"

Vanity sighed again and turned and faced him. "Malcolm,

why are you here? I already told you that it's over between us. If you can't accept friendship between us, then it's best we just not speak anymore!"

"So that's just it, huh?" he asked, staring hard at her. "You just up and say fuck it one night, after all this time, right? Who's the nigga, Vanity?"

"Malcolm, look!"

"Who is he?"

"Malcolm!"

"Who the fuck is he?" Malcolm barked at Vanity, cutting her off.

Vanity stared at Malcolm like he had lost his damn mind. "He's my new man, and that's all you need to know! Move!" she said, losing her cool.

She then pushed Malcolm out of the way and snatched open her car door and climbed inside her Corvette. She cranked up the car and ignored the way Malcolm was staring at her as she backed out of her parking space. She pulled off and headed to the front of her complex, driving out the front gate. Vanity reached over to her purse on the passenger seat, dug out her phone, and called Boss's phone number.

"Yeah!"

"Boss, I need to talk to you."

"What's up?"

"In person, baby."

Boss was quiet for a moment and then finally spoke up: "I'm handling something right now. Can you pick me up in twenty minutes?"

"From where?" Vanity asked as she drove and listened to Boss give her the location where he wanted her to meet him.

\* \* \*

"So, you and Boss are serious already, huh?" Erica asked Brandi as the two of them were putting together the front room while the others were finishing decorating the den the way Boss suggested.

"He says we're serious!" Brandi stated, before she continued after a brief moment, "I believe ReSean really wants to be with me, but something's up with him and Vanity."

"Who?"

"Pleasure!"

"You mean Pleasure from down at the club, Brandi?"

Brandi nodded her head and then sat down on the new cream-colored fur couch. She waited until Erica was seated beside her.

"I think Boss and Vanity met and have been talking, and when I spoke to him about it, he got a little defensive. But then he said he wouldn't disrespect me."

"What about Malcolm White?" Erica asked. "I thought Vanity was talking to him?"

"From how she's been calling, I'm guessing that she either cut Malcolm loose or is playing games, and from the feeling I get from ReSean, I think if Malcolm tries anything, something bad is going to happen. We both saw ReSean the other night at the Bar-B-Q Pit."

"So, what are you going to do?" Erica asked, seeing the start of real worry on Brandi's face, which showed her how much her girl really liked Boss.

Brandi shook her head slowly.

"I'm not really sure, Erica, but I do know I'm not letting ReSean go. I really care for this man, and if Vanity wants to go through it with me for my man, then she has a real big problem!"

* * *

"Who's that?" Eazy asked.

Eazy, Boss, and Rico stood on the front porch of Gina King's house as they watched the candy-apple red drop-top Corvette pull up in front of the house.

Boss stared at the Stingray and watched as the driver's side window slid down, where he recognized Vanity sitting behind the wheel. He turned back to Gina to let her know he was starting a business. He then handed her $500 and explained that Eazy was taking her to his hotel room, and that she would stay there until he and she found a new place for her to stay. He then dapped up with Eazy and Rico.

"I'ma hit y'all up later on. Let me take care of something real quick."

"Be careful, my nigga!" Eazy told Boss.

"No doubt!" Boss replied as he left the porch and walked out to the Corvette and up to the driver's window. "What's good, shorty?"

"You!" Vanity replied, smiling at him. "Get in so we can go."

Boss pushed away from the driver's window and walked around to the passenger side and climbed in. Trey Songz's "Can't Help but Wait" was playing on the radio.

"Hey!" Vanity said, leaning over and kissing Boss on the lips before pulling off.

Vanity was quiet for a few seconds and drove with her right hand resting on his left thigh.

Boss broke the silence and asked, "So what you wanna talk to me about, shorty?"

"Us!" she answered, glancing over to Boss. "Boss, I can't lie anymore. Since day one when we first met and you came over to sit next to me on the Greyhound bus, I knew then that I wanted something with you. I just said we could be friends because I didn't want you thinking I was some thirsty ho, but I don't care now, Boss. I want you to be my man!"

Boss chuckled lightly and shook his head. "What's up with that nigga Malcolm?" he then asked.

"I ended it with Malcolm, Boss," she admitted, pulling to a stop at a red light and looking over at him. "I want you, Boss! I don't know what it is about you, but I want you to be my man."

Boss shook his head and admitted, "Shorty, I'm feeling you and you know that, but I just started kicking it with someone."

"Who?" Vanity asked, catching an instant attitude. "You fucking that bitch Strawberry, Boss?"

"Naw, ma!" Boss answered, smirking at her jealousy on display. "I'm with Brandi."

"Hold up!" Vanity cried out loudly.

Horns began to blow from the cars behind her. She looked up to see that the traffic light was green.

Vanity pulled off from the light only to pull over and turn into a BP gas station. She parked the car beside the air pump and then turned back to Boss.

"Boss, please tell me you're not messing with the same Brandi that dances at the Pink Palace with me? You fucking that bitch Privilege, Boss?"

"Vanity, relax!"

"No, Boss! I'm not relaxing!" Vanity told him. "Answer

my question. Are you fucking her or not?"

"Does it matter?" Boss inquired.

"Don't play with me, Boss! Answer the question!"

"Yeah!"

"Yeah what?"

"Yeah, we did something."

Vanity stared at Boss a few minutes and held his eyes.

"I want my time, Boss. I want my time now!"

"Shorty, you trying to start something, ain't you?" he asked. "You know once Brandi found about—"

"Fuck Brandi!" Vanity told Boss, interrupting him. "I'm not even asking you to leave that bitch, because all that's going to do is make you wanna stay with her ass. I'ma let you decide for yourself who you wanna be with. I only want my time, Boss. Can you give me some of your time?"

Boss stared at Vanity a few moments. "You serious, ain't you?" Boss asked.

Vanity reached over and grabbed his dick and began caressing his manhood. She then leaned over and slid her tongue into his mouth. She broke the kiss after a moment and met his eyes.

"Does that look like I'm playing about us, Boss? Give me just this one thing; and whatever happens, good or bad, I'll accept it."

Boss sighed as he shook his head and then stared out the window for a few moments. "If I agree to this, then I want you to understand that if you step to Brandi at any time, it's done with us."

"I promise!"

"And I want you to find a new club to dance at!"

"I'll start looking tomorrow morning," Vanity replied.

"Anything else?"

Boss shook his head as he looked back over at Vanity and said, "Naw! Nothing else!"

"Good!" Vanity stated as she started the car and pulled off.

"Where we going?" Boss asked as Vanity drove off.

"My place!" she answered, smiling as she began heading back in the direction of her apartment complex.

\* \* \*

Boss made it back to Vanity's apartment complex a short while later and allowed her to lead him to her apartment. Boss barely got fully inside her place when she attacked him, even before shutting and locking the door.

Boss was down to his jeans and Nikes by the time Vanity got him into the front room and pushed him down onto the sofa. Boss allowed her to finish stripping him until he was completely naked. He then sat down as she gave him a slow striptease. He noticed that she had a navel piercing just like Brandi, but Brandi also had a piercing in the lips of her pussy. Vanity's pussy had no piercing, but she was just as bald as Brandi.

"I see you like what you see!" Vanity told him as she climbed up onto Boss's lap and felt his hard dick pressing against her pussy, which caused a moan to escape her lips.

She reached down between Boss's legs and gripped his dick. She sat up and positioned his manhood at her opening, when Boss stopped her just as his cell phone began ringing.

"Hold up, shorty!" Boss said, reaching down and snatching up his jeans from the ground and pulling out a condom and his cell phone. He gave the condom to Vanity and then saw that Eazy was on the end of the line. "What's good, playboy?"

"Bruh, we got that information on ya boy we was talking

86

about!" Eazy told him. "And what's sweet is that we actually staring at this dude right now, my nigga!"

"Where you at?" Boss asked as he pushed Vanity off of his lap and stood up from the sofa. He began getting dressed as Vanity began asking him what was wrong.

Once Eazy and Rico told Boss where they were located, he hung up the phone and looked at a confused Vanity.

"Get dressed! I gotta go. Now!"

# TEN

**EAZY RECOGNIZED THE CORVETTE** Stingray that pulled inside the Wendy's where he and Rico were parked as they watched the Bentley Continental GT Mulliner Coupe that was parked inside the parking lot at Granny B's Soul Food Diner. Eazy tapped Rico and nodded toward the Corvette. Eazy let down Rico's window on the passenger side. He then hit the car horn as soon as Boss climbed from the Stingray, and then waved him over to his Lexus.

"What's good?" Boss asked as he stopped at the passenger window. "Where's this nigga at?"

"Across the street," Rico answered, nodding over to the Bentley. "The Escalade's with the ol' boy too."

"How many?" Boss asked.

"Six went inside the restaurant with Victor, and then you got the driver. He's strapped too," Eazy told Boss.

Boss nodded his head and looked over at the Bentley and the restaurant. "Eazy, I want you with me. Rico, you strapped?"

"Always!" Rico answered, lifting up his shirt to show the .40 caliber that sat inside the front of his jeans.

"Alright. Deal with the driver and then wait for my signal," Boss said with a nod.

"I got you, my nigga!" Rico replied, opening the passenger door as Boss stepped back to let Rico out.

Boss climbed inside the Lexus as Rico disappeared, crossing the street away from the soul food restaurant.

"Let's go have a talk with this Victor White clown, playboy!" Boss said to Eazy.

"That's what the fuck I'm talking about, my nigga!" Eazy stated with a smile.

Eazy then started up his Lexus and backed out of his parking spot.

Boss was deep in his planning. He was trying to put things together inside his mind on how to deal with the issue he and his boys were about to walk into, so he slowly began to smile. He then pulled out his cell phone and sent Rico a quick text.

* * *

Victor White was dining with the women he had met at the hotel where he was staying in Miami. He was there dealing with all the bullshit concerning the murder of his best worker in Miami, and he was trying to figure out who was responsible for putting Prince and Murder Mike in the hospital. However, he received very little information about the guys who robbed him and Prince.

While Victor was listening to something one of the females was saying across the table, he locked eyes on the two young men who entered the restaurant. While Victor kept his gaze on the young man wearing a fitted cap on his head, he set down his fork once the two young men began walking in his direction. He maintained eye contact with the men as Gray, his head of security, stepped forward to block them.

"Mr. White!" Gray said as he stopped beside Victor's table. "You have someone that says he has proof of the guy you're looking for concerning Lucky and both Prince's and Mike's issue."

"Send him over!" Victor told Gray when he looked back at the young man.

After Gray left, Victor White dismissed the women seated across from him as the young man with the fitted cap appeared at his table and sat down without being invited.

"So, you have something to tell me?"

"So, you're Victor White, huh?" Boss asked, smirking as he sat looking over the supposed gangster. "I heard you had a reward for the guy who took care of the clown Lucky and his crew, correct?"

"I'm looking for each man who's behind his murder, as well as the ones responsible for having my men placed inside the hospital and robbing me for over $200,000 and taking my drugs."

"I think you got your information wrong, playboy! There was never more than one person who robbed and killed Lucky and his crew," Boss said, chuckling lightly.

"And how exactly do you know that?" Victor questioned Boss. "Matter of fact, who are you?"

Boss ignored his question but tossed a sack of weed across the table in front of Victor.

"Doesn't that look familiar?" Boss asked.

Victor shifted his eyes and looked down at the sack of weed, which he instantly recognized. He then looked back across the table to the young man. "Where'd you get that from?"

"Lucky!" Boss answered with a smirk. "I'm the one that sent Lucky where he's at now. So again, I'm asking. You was looking for me? I'm right here."

Victor stared at the young man in front of him who claimed to be responsible for the problems he was dealing with as well as the missing money and drugs.

"You either must be extremely stupid or ready to die!" Victor said as he calmly picked up the sack of weed and looked it over.

"It was nice meeting you!" Boss stated, cutting off Victor.

Boss then stood up from his seat and simply walked away from the table and Victor. Victor watched as the young man and his friend walked out of the restaurant. He then nodded to Gray, who instantly followed behind the two men with three of his own for backup.

After Gray left the restaurant, Victor tossed the sack of weed back onto the table and then stood from his seat, which caused the rest of his security team to stand up as well. Victor then started for the door, leaving the restaurant without finishing his meal. Once they were all outside and walking toward his Bentley, Victor called his brother on his cell phone. Victor then climbed into the backseat of his car along with two of his security guards.

"Hello!" Victor said, recognizing his brother's voice. "I found the muthafucker who's been causing all the trouble out here. Listen to this though. It supposedly was some young nigga that killed Lucky and robbed us."

"How'd you find this out?"

"Because the muthafucker showed up at my table at Granny B's while I was eating," Victor informed his brother in disgust. "The bastard admitted everything and even showed me some of the weed we were giving Lucky."

"Is this problem being taken care of?"

"Gray is at this very moment! What the hell!" Victor yelled, after the Bentley jerked to a hard stop, almost throwing him from his seat.

He straightened himself inside his seat and looked up front just in time to see the driver shut the car door after climbing out from behind the steering wheel.

"What in the hell!"

Victor was confused a moment while watching the driver walk away from the Bentley, only to see a Lexus slowly pull up and the driver stop at the other driver's window. Victor tried opening the car door, only to find the door locked and unable to be opened.

"What the hell is going on? What's wrong with my fucking door?"

Victor heard his phone begin ringing, realizing that he must have hung up on his brother.

"Hello!" Victor answered, expecting to hear his brother's voice.

"Mr. White!" Gray said.

"Where the hell are you?" Victor yelled, looking back out his window.

He froze when his eyes locked in on what he was seeing.

"Sir, we lost the two guys from the restaurant. They somehow got—!"

Victor dropped the phone from his hand as he sat staring at the same young man who was just at the soul food restaurant only a short while ago. He was now standing outside the Lexus and smoking what looked like a blunt. Victor shifted his eyes to the two other men who were now approaching the Bentley with guns in hand.

"Get me the hell outta here!" Victor shouted while pushing both his security guards so he could get across the front seat behind the steering wheel.

Victor stared back out the window frozen in complete terror. He was only able to take his last breath when he turned around and looked back at the Lexus with the young man with the fitted cap. Just then, the window exploded and bullets rained down on him and his men.

# ELEVEN

**BOSS MADE IT BACK** to the house and saw that Brandi and her girls' cars were still at the house. He waited until Eazy parked his Lexus in front of the house, since the driveway was crowded. He then climbed out, with Eazy and Rico following behind him.

As Boss walked up the walkway, he looked over at Rico, whose phone had been ringing. Boss then stepped up onto the porch, unlocked the door, and opened the front door.

"Damn!" Eazy said as soon as he stepped into the house behind Boss. "Something smells good as hell up in here!"

"Excuse me, young man!" Evelyn said, stepping out of the kitchen. "What did you just say, Erick?"

"Momma!" Eazy said in surprise, just as Tina and Regina exited the kitchen. "Mom, what are you doing here?"

"My baby called and told your father and me about ReSean's new house, and your father just took Erica, Brandi, and Maxine off to the store to pick up some stuff we need to finish cooking."

"Mrs. Collins."

"ReSean, don't you dare call me Mrs. Collins, not one more time!" Evelyn told Boss, cutting him off while smiling. "You either can call me momma or Evelyn. Your decision."

Boss smiled at the show of affection by Evelyn Collins.

"Momma, is Mr. Collins barbecuing?"

"He sure is!" Evelyn answered, but then took Boss's hand, led him into the den, and had him sit down on the sofa. "I want you to sit here and relax until Brandi gets back. I want you two to talk, because you two have a lot to talk about. Are we understood?"

"Yes, ma'am!" Boss answered, smiling up at her.

"You two come and stop staring at my son!" Evelyn told Tina and Regina as she led them out of the den so Boss and Eazy could spend time together.

Eazy shook his head at his mother, with Tina and Regina following behind her. He then sat down across from Boss and nodded at the PlayStation 4.

"You wouldn't happen to have some Madden 24, would you?"

"What do you think?" Boss asked while smirking at Eazy. "You trying to go in or what?"

Eazy dug out his bankroll and peeled off two $100 bills and set them on top of the glass coffee table.

"So, what's up? You trying to lose some money or what?" Eazy asked afterward.

"Whoa!" Rico said as he walked into the den and saw Boss dig out his phat bankroll from his pocket. "What's the deal in here?"

"Eazy's trying to lose $200 to me in some Madden 24!" Boss told Rico as he set down his two $100 bills on top of the coffee table, only for Rico to want a part of the bet as well.

* * *

Brandi broke out in a smile at the sight of Eazy's Lexus in front of the house. She almost pushed Erica out of the car once Mr. Collins came to a stop. Once she was out of the car, she and Maxine grabbed a few bags from the backseat. She then started walking toward the door, only to hear Mr. Collins yell for her to tell Eazy to come outside and grab the rest of the bags.

Once she opened the front door, she heard Wale and Usher's "Matrimony" as well as Boss and his boys yelling and laughing. Brandi couldn't help but smile at the sound of her man's voice. She first stopped in the kitchen to drop off the bags she was carrying, and caught the look her godmother shot her as she was leaving.

Brandi approached the den and saw Boss sitting on the La-Z-Boy, with both Eazy and Rico sitting on the sofa playing PlayStation. Brandi walked up beside Boss and quickly caught his attention.

"Time out!" Boss said, after seeing Brandi walk into the den while in the middle of picking his play. He pulled her onto his lap and kissed her, tonguing her down. Afterward, he wrapped his arms around her. "Alright. Time in!"

Brandi smiled as she lay into Boss wrapping her arms around his neck loosely. She then looked at the flat-screen television and watched the Atlantic Falcons and Miami Dolphins playing on the screen. "ReSean, who's winning?"

"He is!" Rico answered while staring hard at the flat-screen as he and Rico played defense against Boss."

"You winning, babe?" Brandi asked, kissing Boss on the neck.

"They thought shit was sweet, ma!" Boss told Brandi with a smile. "They play on the same team against the boys, shorty. And they're still losing!"

"I know one thing!" Darrell Collins said, drawing everyone's attention to him by the tone of his voice. "All of those bags out inside the car won't get inside by themselves, so you guys need to put that game down and get those bags inside this house!"

Brandi felt a pat on her butt from Boss for her to get up

from his lap. She smiled as Boss, Eazy, and Rico put down their controllers and left the den to do as they were told. She then looked up at Mr. Collins and saw the way he was looking at her.

"What?" she asked.

"Young lady, you need to get yourself inside that kitchen with Evelyn and those other girls. That kitchen is big enough for all of you!" Darrell told his goddaughter.

"Yes, sir!" Brandi replied, leaving the den and passing Mr. Collins while catching the small smile on his lips as he stood watching her.

* * *

Boss stepped outside onto the back pool and patio area where Mr. Collins was barbecuing on the stone grill. Boss walked over and handed Darrell the Corona that he brought out for him.

"Thanks, son!" Darrell told Boss, with a smile.

After taking a deep pull from the beer bottle, Darrell looked at Boss and asked, "ReSean, tell me something, son. What exactly are your plans? Why are you really in Miami, since I hear you're from Atlanta?"

"Truthfully, Mr. Collins," Boss started.

Boss looked off a moment and then back at Eazy's father. He then began explaining about his problems with his mother's husband and even about his mother's lies she told him to get him to live in Miami with his supposed birth father, whom he only met once at the age of four or five. However, he admitted that his mother decided her husband was more important to her than he was.

"So basically, you're out here by yourself with no family. Is that what you're telling me, son?" Darrell asked Boss, once the young man was finished telling his story.

"Pretty much, sir!" Boss answered. "But it's fine. I plan on being fine, sir! My mother may not believe in me or what I want to do, but I'm going to be good!"

"I don't doubt that, son!" Darrell told Boss truthfully, just as the patio door opened and Brandi, Erica, Eazy, and the others all walked outside.

"Honey!" Evelyn said as she walked up beside her husband. "Everything's finished, and we're just waiting on the meat."

"It's about done," Darrell stated as he nodded to the pan covered with clear plastic wrap that was filled with ribs, grilled chicken, steak, and hamburgers. "There's some meat there! You can all start eating now if you all want to."

"We'll all eat together," Evelyn told her husband.

"Boss!" Rico called, getting his attention and motioning him over away from the others.

"What's good, Rico?" Boss asked, after leaving Brandi's side to see what he wanted, only for Rico to hold out his cell phone to him.

"Who's this?" Boss inquired.

"That's April!" Rico told Boss. "She's the pill connect, my nigga."

Boss took the phone and placed it to his ear. He looked back at Brandi and saw her laughing with Maxine and the rest of the girls.

"Hello!" Boss said.

"Hello! Am I speaking with whom I'm told goes by the name of Boss?"

"That's correct, April."

"So, tell me, Boss, how can I be of assistance?"

"How about we meet in person and discuss this further?" Boss suggested. "I'd rather not talk business over the phone, and I would rather we meet in person."

"Okay, Boss," April agreed. "When would you like to meet?"

Boss was finishing up his phone call with April after they set up a time and day for the two of them to meet. Boss locked eyes with Brandi while he was speaking on the phone, and she was watching him. He winked his eye at her and then motioned her over. Once he finished his phone call and hung up, Boss called to Rico and tossed him back his cell phone.

"Ma, look! I'm not really into explaining myself, but I'm trying to show and prove to you that I'm with you. That wasn't Vanity on the phone. It was April. Rico's pill connect," Boss told Brandi.

"So, you're into pills, too?"

"Something like that."

"What does that mean?"

"I sell blue devils, shorty," Boss lightly laughed.

"Blue what?" Brandi asked him, with a confused look on her face.

"It's both roxies and cocaine mixed together, shorty!" Boss told her. "I crush up roxies and mix them with power, and then put the mix inside blue pill capsules."

"So that's what you were selling the other night at the Bar-B-Q Pit when Smoker Berry and those people were all crowded around you?"

"Pretty much."

"So, answer one last thing."

"Alright."

"That night at the Bar-B-Q Pit, when you and Eazy got into it with Grip and Cash, there was that shooting a little while later. On the news it showed that not only Lucky and all his boys were found dead, but a few minutes ago we were watching the news and Victor White was found dead inside his Bentley by the old warehouses off of I-95, and everybody knows Lucky worked for Victor. He was supposedly in town trying to find out what happened to Lucky, his money, and his drugs—and now he's also dead. You know what, ReSean, I know the answer to my question without having to ask just from the smirk on your face. So I'll just say this! Make sure you come home every night. That's all I ask you."

"I will. You got that, shorty?" Boss asked her, wrapping his arms her five-foot-two frame and kissing her lips as she lifted her head to kiss him.

* * *

Malcolm couldn't believe what the fuck he was listening to as he sat inside his den watching the six o'clock news on Fox. He sat listening to the correspondent reporting about the murder of known drug dealer Victor White, who was the younger brother of known drug lord Travis White. Malcolm shook his head in confusion on what the hell was going on. He thought about Lucky's murder and his whole crew; then the murder of Pam, Cash's younger sister; and now Victor White.

"What the fuck is going on around here?" Malcolm asked out loud, just as Moses entered the den.

"Your pops is on the phone," Moses told Malcolm, handing him the cell phone that he brought inside the den.

Malcolm sighed loudly when he took the phone from Moses, already knowing what he was about to hear from his father. Malcolm then took a breath, and after releasing it, he placed the phone up to his ear.

"Yeah, Pops! What's up?"

"You mind telling me exactly what's going on in my city?" Malcolm Sr. asked. "What's this with Victor White being murdered in my city?"

"Pops, I'm trying to figure all of that—!"

"You trying to what?" Malcolm Sr. stated, cutting off his son. "Explain to me how it's that you're unable to tell me what's going on in my city? I left you all the keys to run the city, and you're telling me you have no idea what's going on! Find out who's responsible for what the fuck is going on inside my city, and I want to know soon, Malcolm! Are we clear?"

Malcolm never got a chance to respond to his father, hearing him hang up on him. Malcolm caught himself before throwing the phone across the room. Instead, he just tossed the phone onto the coffee table and sighed loudly in utter confusion and aggravation.

\* \* \*

Brandi stared at the mirror inside the master bedroom of Boss's new rental house. She took a deep breath to calm her nerves, as she was surprised at how nervous she was just from the thought of what she was about to do with Boss.

Brandi sighed again as she pushed away from the sink. She then walked over to the shut bathroom door, opened it, and walked out into the dimly lit bedroom. She made her way over to the bed and was about to climb in, pausing when she noticed that Boss was already asleep. After shaking her head and smiling at the sight before her, Brandi picked up the remote and shut off the flat-screen television. She then climbed into bed beside Boss, covered him, and lay beside him. Just as she put her head on his chest, she noticed the red blinking light on his phone. Brandi stared a few minutes at the blinking light before she ignored it, shut her eyes, and got some sleep.

# TWELVE

**BOSS WAS UP EARLY** the next morning. He showered and got dressed in metallic blue True Religion jeans, a white Hanes T-shirt, a pair of Timberlands, and a tan blazer-style leather coat. Boss then grabbed his keys, money, and his .45 from the dresser next to the bed, just as Brandi called his name. Boss looked over at her as she lay awake watching him. Boss walked around the bed to her side as she rolled over to face him. He sat down beside her.

"Sorry about last night. I know I fell asleep on you."

"It's okay," she told him as she leaned over and kissed him. "What are you about to do today?"

"I've got a few things to handle, and I gotta meet April later today," Boss told Brandi, brushing her hair back out of her face.

"Will I see you later?" Brandi asked him.

"Hit me up later on," he told her.

He then kissed her again before standing up from the bed and walking over to his dresser. He picked up an all-white Yankees cap, slid it onto his head, and then winked at Brandi, which caused her to smile before he left the bedroom.

Boss walked out the front door a few minutes later and locked the door behind him. He then walked over to his Porsche, hit the locks, and walked toward the driver's door. He dug out his phone from its case at his waist and then dug out his Newports before climbing into the car. As he started the car, he called Eazy's phone and then lit his cigarette. He then backed out of the driveway just as Eazy answered his phone.

"Hello!"

"You still asleep, playboy?"

"Yeah! What's up though?"

"I'm on my way to your crib now. Get dressed!"

"I'm not at the house, bruh. I'm at Erica's spot."

"Well, get ready! I'll be there in a few minutes."

"Yeah, whatever!"

After hanging up with Eazy, Boss then called Rico's number next.

"Yeah!" Rico answered after three rings.

"What's up, playboy? You still in bed, too?"

"It's 7:45 a.m., Boss. What the fuck do I need to get up so early for?"

"Money, nigga!" Boss answered. "Get up and be ready when Eazy and me get to your crib."

"Yeah, alright."

Boss shook his smile after hanging up with Rico. He realized he had a lot of work to do to get both his boys on the same page, if he was to truly move his business to where he wanted it to go.

* * *

Boss made it to Erica's apartment thirty minutes later after stopping and getting breakfast. He parked the Porsche and then carried the food to her front door. He knocked loud enough to be heard through the apartment.

"Hey, Boss!" Erica said a few moments later, smiling as she opened up the front door and greeted him.

"What's up, cutie?" Boss said, kissing her cheek before entering the apartment.

"Eazy's in the bathroom," Erica told Boss as she closed and locked the front door.

"Hey, how long have you known Brandi?" Boss asked as he handed Erica a bag of food for her and Eazy.

"A little longer than I've known Eazy, why?" Erica asked as she walked into the kitchen.

Boss followed her but stopped at the counter with his food.

"It's just that I'm feeling, shorty. But at the same time, I'm trying to get shit right with the shit I got going on with Eazy and Rico, and I'm sure ya know my story. So, if I fuck up, I'm on the streets, just as my mom actually intended me to be. What I'm really saying is that I'm really trying to kick it with Brandi, but she's trying to take it to the next level, and I'm still on the first level while I'm about to turn up out in these streets. How do I make shorty understand that?"

"Have you tried just telling her, Boss?"

"That's it there! I know if I tell shorty, she's gonna think I'm on some shorty's shit!"

"So basically, what you're asking me to do is talk to Brandi for you, right?"

"Something like that!" Boss replied, just as Eazy walked into the kitchen.

"What's up, my nigga?" Eazy said, dapping up with Boss before walking over to the refrigerator.

"Boss brought breakfast," Erica told her man, handing him his food from the plastic bag.

Eazy thanked Erica, kissed her on the cheek, and then walked over to stand beside Boss at the counter.

"So, what's up? You got at Rico yet?" Eazy questioned.

"He's waiting on us to pick him up," Boss told Eazy, only for Erica to call to Eazy.

"What's up, baby?" he replied, looking back at her.

"Are you still going to be able to pick me up today from

work?" she asked Eazy. "Remember, I'm supposed to take my car to the shop today."

"What time you gotta take your ride in, Erica?"

"I can take it in this morning if it's easier. But I don't know how long it'll be there, Eazy."

"We can take care of that," Boss spoke up, drawing both Eazy's and Erica's eyes to him. He looked back to Erica and asked, "You know how to drive a stick shift, shorty?"

"Yeah, why?" Erica asked.

"We'll follow you to the auto shop, and afterward you can drive my ride to do you until your wheels get right," Boss explained.

"What about you, Boss?" Erica asked.

"I'ma be good, shorty," Boss told her, winking his eye at her.

* * *

Vanity hung up the phone with the owner of the Pink Palace after just informing him that she was leaving. She then called a friend she knew in Miami Beach at Club Climax.

"Yolanda Scott."

"Yolanda, it's Vanity. You busy?"

"Vanity! Hey, girl! I'm only busy if you're still not willing to take up my offer to be my headliner at my club."

"That's why I'm calling now," Vanity told Yolanda. "If you've still got an opening and—"

"When can you start?" Yolanda asked, cutting her off.

"I can start tonight or whenever."

"I'll tell you what, Vanity. Why don't you come in tonight and just see how the place is, and you can start this Thursday."

"Okay, I'll be in around nine or ten o'clock," Vanity replied. "You mind if I bring a friend?"

"Another dancer?"

"No, it's my man!"

"Be my guest," Yolanda replied. "I'll see you tonight, and just let the doorman know who you are once you get here."

"I'll see you later," Vanity stated before she hung up the phone.

Vanity sat on her sofa and stared at the television screen thinking about what she was actually doing for Boss. She found herself smiling and ended up calling him.

"Yeah!" Boss answered in the middle of the second ring.

"Hey, babe, where you at?"

"Handling business with my nigga Eazy. What's up though?"

"I wanna see you if you got the time."

"Let me handle this one thing, and then you can pick me up at the hotel off of 27th Avenue beside the Dolphin Stadium."

"You gonna call me?"

"Naw! Just meet me there in ten minutes, shorty."

"Alright, babe!"

After hanging up the phone with Boss, Vanity smiled and quickly jumped up from the couch. She rushed to the bedroom to begin getting ready to go see her future man.

* * *

Vanity was dressed in a Dolce & Gabbana outfit she knew showed all her most curvaceous parts. She was pulling inside the hotel she was meeting Boss at almost twelve minutes later than the ten minutes he told her to be there to pick him up. She pulled out her phone and called him.

"Yeah!" Boss answered at the start of the second ring.

"Hey, baby, I'm outside."

"Alright. I'm on my way out."

Once she hung up the phone, she smiled and could feel her heart speeding up while she was waiting for him to exit the hotel. She heard her phone ring, so she picked it up even though it was Malcolm calling her.

"What, Malcolm?" she answered after sighing loudly and deeply.

"So that's how you answer the phone now, huh?"

"Last time I checked, this was my phone, right?"

"Whatever, Vanity! Where you at though?"

"I'm waiting on someone."

"Who?"

"None of your business, Malcolm!" Vanity told him at the same time she saw Boss, Eazy, and a Spanish-looking guy walking out of the hotel together.

She broke out in a smile again.

"Malcolm, look, call me later. I gotta go!" she said into the phone.

After ending her call with Malcolm, who was still yelling at her when she hung up, she let down her window and called out to get the attention of Boss and his boys. She saw her boo motion for her to hold on, so she sat watching him talk and dap with the guys. After they were done, he finally made his way over to her Corvette.

"What's up, shorty?" Boss said as he climbed into her Stingray.

Vanity smiled at him as she pulled off her Dolce & Gabbana shades, leaned over, and slid her tongue into his mouth. "I missed you, handsome!"

"Oh really?"

"Don't sound like you don't believe me. I'm the one out here chasing behind your butt!" she joked.

"I see it, shorty!" Boss told her, shooting a small smirk at her.

"That's good to hear!" Vanity replied, smiling as she playfully rolled her eyes at him before putting her shades back on. She then pulled off and started toward the exit. "Where's your car at?"

"I let a friend use it," Boss explained as he pulled an already rolled blunt from behind his ear under his fitted cap.

"Hold on!" Vanity said, looking from the road over to Boss. "You telling me you're out here catching rides with other people when I know you can afford to buy two cars, boo!"

"What makes you so sure I'm able to afford two rides, shorty?" Boss asked as he lit up the blunt he held up to his lips.

"Boss, come on!" Vanity told him, glancing back over at him. "I pay attention to you, and from the time you got here in Miami to now, you not only have a Porsche but somehow also keep a pocketful of money. And I've even seen you try to slip what looked like a baggy with a blue pill inside of it back into your pocket back at the club. I'm pretty sure you're selling pills, aren't you?"

"I see you're pay attention more than I thought!" Boss stated while also ignoring Vanity's question.

Vanity caught the way Boss ignored her question, but she didn't mention it. "What types of cars do you like, boo? I see you like Porsches, but what about Ferraris?" she asked.

"Hell yeah!" Boss replied as he handed over the blunt to Vanity. "You know somebody selling one?"

Vanity smiled when she saw how excited Boss was about the Ferrari. "Don't think I'm crazy, but there's this guy who's a regular customer of mine at the club. I did a few parties with some girls for him, and I know he's selling a Ferrari. You wanna see it?"

"How's it look?"

"It looks almost brand new, babe!"

Boss thought a few moments, slowly nodded his head, and then said, "Yeah, let's check the thing out!"

# THIRTEEN

**BRANDI SAW BOSS'S PORSCHE** parked in front of the barber/beauty shop that her cousin and her girl Erica owned. She parked her Aston Martin, grabbed her purse, and climbed from the car. As she exited and entered the shop, she waved to her cousin, Tim, but continued walking around to the beauty shop side.

"Hey, Brandi, girl!"

Brandi waved to a few of the customers and girls working in the shop she recognized, and then she walked back to Erica's station, where she was taking care of a client's hair.

"Hey, girl!" Erica said with a smile as she paused working on her client to give a hug to Brandi.

"I see you got a lot of heads already," Brandi said, seeing all the women already waiting on Erica. "So, what's up? What you need to talk to me about?"

"Hold on!" Erica told Brandi. She then asked the woman in her seat to give her a few minutes, turning back to Brandi and motioning her to the back office. Once the two of them were inside the back room and Erica locked the office door, she turned around, walked over, and sat down on the edge of the desk facing Brandi. "Boss asked me to talk to you."

"Wait! What?" Brandi asked. "What does ReSean want you to talk to me about, Erica?"

"Brandi, calm down!" Erica told her friend. "Look, Boss really does like you and does want to continue seeing you, but you have to understand that even though he's young, he still has his own life he is trying to build. Brandi, don't push him into anything too serious, because he's really focused on getting his self together. You understand what I'm telling you?"

"Let me get this straight!" Brandi stated with an attitude. "ReSean told you all that bullshit when he could really just tell me he didn't wanna be with me himself?"

"Brandi! Boss didn't say he didn't—!"

"Erica, why would my supposed man need you to talk to me when he could have just talked to me himself? Make me understand that!"

"You see how you're reacting?" Erica said. "Boss figured you would act like this, which is why he asked me to talk to you since we're friends. All that man is trying to get you to understand is that he wants to be with you, but he wants you to slow down a little."

"Slow down, huh?" Brandi repeated with a nod of her head. "Alright! I'ma give his ass all he wants."

Erica watched Brandi angrily leave the office. Erica then stood up from her desk and walked back to her station.

* * *

Boss pulled out his ringing phone as he and Vanity were walking out of the jewelry store, where she bought him a brand-new white gold Cuban-link chain with a Jesus face piece. Boss saw Erica calling as Vanity was leading him into another store. "Yeah! What's good, Erica?"

"Boss, I spoke with Brandi."

"And?"

"And like you said, she got pissed after I told her about what you and I talked about. She's probably gonna call you."

"I think she's calling me now! Hold on!" Boss told Erica, after hearing his phone beep.

He looked on the screen, only to see Eazy calling him.

"Erica, let me hit you back, shorty. That's your man calling."

"Alright, Boss."

After hanging up, Boss switched lines over to Eazy. "What's up, playboy?"

"Boss, we got a problem, my nigga!"

"Tell me about it!" he inquired.

Boss then stood watching Vanity while listening to Eazy tell him about dropping off Rico at the new spot out in Opa-locka only to receive a call from him five minutes later. Rico explained that the dude named Cook and his crew showed up and robbed him and his young assistant, Magic, who was helping him.

"Where you at?" Boss asked as he walked over to Vanity and the hard-smiling salesclerk.

Boss motioned shorty to hurry so they could leave. He then told Eazy to pick up Rico and his boy and then meet him back at the spot. Boss then hung up the phone. "Shorty, we gotta go!" he yelled to Vanity.

"Alright!" Vanity said, seeing the expression on Boss's handsome face.

Once they were outside the mall and entering the parking lot, Boss led Vanity out to his newly purchased metallic blue 2007 Ferrari F430 Spider convertible coupe. He hit the key remote unlocking the doors and walked around to the driver's side as Vanity climbed inside the passenger side.

Boss got inside the Ferrari and started up the car just as his phone started up again. He was backing out of his parking spot as he pulled out his phone and answered it.

"Yeah?"

"ReSean, where are you?"

Boss recognized Brandi's voice and said, "Brandi, let me hit you back, ma. I gotta handle something right now. You at the house?"

"No. I'm at my own place," she spit out at him. "Just make sure you call me when you finish your supposed business!"

"Yeah!" Boss replied, and then hung up the phone. "Shorty, I'ma drop you off back at your spot."

"For what?" Vanity asked him. "Why go way out of the way when we can just go to wherever you need to be? I'll just wait in the car while you handle your business. And I'm not asking, because it wasn't a request."

Boss cut his eyes over to Vanity and actually smirked at her sassiness. He saw no reason to respond, so he shifted gears and punched the gas in the Ferrari, feeling the exotic car jerk and then raise up as it lurched forward.

\* \* \*

"Where the fuck is Boss at?" Rico yelled angrily as he and Eazy sat in the Lexus at the corner of 135th Street in Opa-locka.

"Relax, my nigga!" Eazy told Rico. "My dude says he's coming. He's should be here in a—"

"What the fuck!" Rico yelled, staring out Eazy's window at the Ferrari pulling up beside them.

He wanted to reach for his burner, but he quickly remembered it wasn't there. He watched as the passenger window slid down.

"What the fuck!" Eazy said in surprise at seeing Pleasure in the seat of the Ferrari, not when he saw Boss behind the steering wheel.

Boss climbed out of the car and walked around to the Lexus while the chick from Pink Palace climbed out and walked around and got behind the wheel.

"What's the deal, fellas?" Boss asked as he stopped in front of the driver's door of the Lexus.

"Bruh, I'm ready to murder all these muthafuckers!" Rico said, heated, spitting each word.

"They're still at the spot now?" Boss asked.

"Yeah!" Eazy answered. "We drove past, and they were still there getting money and selling the blue devils Rico and Magic were selling."

"Where's Magic now?" Boss questioned.

"He just slid back up the street to peep at what was going on," Eazy replied.

Boss was quiet for a minute and then looked to his right back toward the main street.

"I got a plan, but, Rico, you're taking the lead with your boy Magic!" Boss said, looking back at Eazy and Rico.

"I'm with that right there!" Rico stated. "We got one problem though, big homie. Those niggas hit me and Magic up for our bangers."

"I want my shit back!" Boss said as he pulled his own .45 from his waist and handed it over to Rico.

\* \* \*

Rico filled Magic in on the plan that Boss came up with as the two of them walked back onto the block on which their trap house was located. Rico stared at the house and saw the crowd out in front waiting in line for blue devils. As they approached the house, they saw the nigga Cook and four of his boys out on the porch of Gina King's. That's when Rico and Magic made their move and pushed through the crowd, headed for the porch.

"Look at this muthafucker!" one of the four guys said when he saw Rico and Magic. He tapped Cook and said, "This nigga really must be stupid as fuck!"

"What the fuck is you doing here!"

Rico pulled the .45 that Boss had given him. He swung up the hammer and pointed it at Cook, whose eyes got huge in both surprise and then in complete terror right before Rico pulled the trigger.

*Boom! Boom!*

Rico ignored the screams and all the people rushing and running to get away after putting two in Cook's face. He then heard more shooting as two of Cook's boys hit the ground with either their chest or face opened up. He swung his .45 at one of the staring guys and put two to his chest, which sent him slamming back into the wall. Rico then dumped another round to his face, erasing his expression.

"Let's go!" Boss yelled, grabbing Rico's arm and pulling him away from the dude he just bodied.

Rico followed Boss and Magic out of the front yard and saw Eazy in the Lexus waiting in front of the house with the engine still running. Rico and Magic hopped inside the back while Boss jumped up front, just as Eazy peeled off from in front of the trap house.

\* \* \*

Eazy made it to the Quickie Mart three minutes from the spot after dealing with Cook and his team. He swung his Lexus into the parking lot where Vanity was already waiting. Boss hopped out of the Lexus and yelled to Eazy to head back to his place as he jogged around to the passenger side of his Ferrari. After hopping inside, Vanity backed out and sped off behind the Lexus.

"Babe, you okay?" Vanity asked Boss, looking over at him a brief moment before focusing back on the road.

"Yeah!" Boss answered. "I'ma keep the gun, but I'ma get you another one. This shit got bodies on it now, and I don't want you with it."

"Do what you think is best, boo!" Vanity told him, even though she had had that same .38 for almost four years now.

Boss was quiet the rest of the way until they reached Eazy's apartment. Boss waited until Vanity parked the Ferrari and they climbed out. He then waited for her to lock up and then walk over to him wrapping her arms around his waist. He dropped his arm around her shoulders as the two of them entered the apartment building and headed up to Eazy's place.

Boss and Vanity entered the apartment a few minutes later, and saw Rico and Magic in the front room while Eazy was somewhere in the back. Boss led Vanity around to the couch and sat down beside her

"You two good?" Boss addressed Rico and Magic.

"Yeah!" both Rico and Magic answered at the same time, before Rico added, "Where the hell did you come from, dawg? I ain't even see you show up."

"You weren't supposed to, playboy!" Boss told Rico, just as he saw Eazy enter the room talking on his cell phone and motioning for everyone to be quiet.

Boss assumed Eazy was on the phone with Erica, so he dug out his Newports and pulled one out from the pack.

"That was Erica," Eazy told Boss after he hung up the phone. "She was asking if I was with you, because somebody's looking for you, my nigga."

"Brandi?" Boss questioned, even after catching the quick shift in Eazy's eyes toward Vanity. "Vanity already knows about Brandi."

Eazy nodded his head and then changed the subject. "What are we gonna do about the spot now, my nigga? We just handled that, and I know it's hot as fuck back that way. How we supposed to handle business with the heat on?"

"Relax!" Boss told him, seeing the same concerned expression on both Rico's and Magic's faces. "I already been thinking about that, and I'ma get at Gina and have her check out the spot, holla at the police, and clear up that her house was taken by some men and that she even reported it and nothing happened."

"Bruh, that sounds good and all, but she's a smoker, even if she's trying to change now," Eazy told Boss. "Police ain't gonna wanna hear that shit from no smoker."

"I'll go with her," Vanity spoke up, drawing everyone's attention to her while she stared at Boss. "If the police won't believe her, then I'll be with her to back up whatever story you come up with, babe. Just tell me what you want me to say."

Boss nodded his head slowly, holding shorty's eyes before he winked at her, which caused Vanity to smile back at him.

"Alright, we'll let Vanity take care of Gina and the police, and I'll take care of explaining to Gina what's going on. Also, I want to get rid of the piece I gave Rico and the .38 I'm holding and get something else. You niggas know somebody who can handle that for me?"

"Babe, I know someone," Vanity spoke up again.

"Damn, Boss, my nigga!" Magic said, smiling as he sat staring at Vanity. "Where the fuck you found baby girl from? She's bad as hell, and she's ready to hold you down to add to the sexiness. She got a sister?"

"Sorry!" Vanity answered, smiling back at Boss. "I only got two older brothers, and I belong to Boss!"

Boss chuckled as he shook his head while Vanity lay against his chest smiling. He looked back over at Eazy and caught the questioning look his boy was giving him.

* * *

Boss first took care of things with Eazy and then Rico and Magic, and then he dealt with Gina and Vanity, where he left the two women to talk and deal with the police back at Gina's house. Boss then drove toward Brandi's condo, but he called her phone to let her know he was on his way.

"You finally decided to call me back?" Brandi asked with an attitude after answering the phone.

"I'm on my way to your place now," Boss told her, ignoring what she just asked him.

"Don't even bother," Brandi responded. "I'm not home."

"Where you at?"

"Out!"

"Where at?"

"Out!"

"So, we playing this game now, huh?"

"I should be asking you that!" Brandi spit back at him. "What type of man sends a woman to deal with his problems? You can't be man enough to tell me straight up that you don't want to be with me, nigga?"

"Brandi, what are you talking about?" Boss asked and sat waiting for an answer.

After pausing a moment with no response, he looked at the screen and realized she had hung up on him. He began calling her back, but stopped himself after he thought about it a minute. "Fuck it!" Boss said as he picked up his phone to call Vanity.

"Hey, babe!"

"How's everything?"

"Gina's talking with the detective who's in charge of the investigation."

"Have you spoken with him yet?"

"He spoke with me first. Everything is going fine," Vanity explained. "Am I seeing you again today or is my time up for today?"

"When you finish, just come by my place," Boss told her, and then gave Vanity the address where he lived and the code to the front gate.

"I'll see you in a few minutes, handsome," Vanity told him before hanging up the phone.

After hanging up with Vanity, Boss made one last call, pushing in the number he knew from memory.

"Who's this?"

"Murphy, what's good, playboy? This is Boss."

"Boss? My young hustler, Boss?"

"There's only one of me, my nigga!"

"What's up, youngin'? I heard you left town."

"Yeah! I'm out here in Miami," Boss told his old cocaine connect. "I wanna holla at you about some business though."

"That's nothing new! What's up though, youngin'?"

Boss explained in code to Murphy, which they both spoke, and let him know he wanted to buy at least five bricks of whole cocaine from him. Boss then asked if the prices were still the same.

"Alright, youngin'," Murphy said with a little laugh. "You know I fuck with you heavy, and you've been fucking with me since you was a bad-ass lil' shorty. Them things go for thirty now, but since you're family, I'ma give it to you for twenty a brick. You good with that?"

Boss did some quick math inside his head and smiled. "Alright! That's a deal, playboy. I'ma be up there in a few days," Boss informed him.

"I'll have that ready for you. Just let me know when you're on your way, youngin'," Murphy said.

"I got you!" Boss replied. "Hey, what's up with my boy Trigger? I tried to hit him up to give him my new number, but his phone cut off."

"Youngin', your boy's locked up," Murphy told Boss. "He just caught two months in the county. But he got like a week left since I hear the judge ran that probation time he did out here with the time he caught, and now he's about to jump back out."

Boss smiled at the news that he just received and then said, "Murphy, do your boy a favor. I'ma send some cash out to you for my boy Trigger, and I want you to put some on my nigga's commissary and then have one of your girls take my nigga shopping. Then send his ass down here to me. Let him know I'ma be waiting on his ass!"

"I got you, youngin'!" Murphy told Boss before hanging up the phone.

Boss smiled as he sat inside his car that was parked in his driveway back at his house. He shut off the Ferrari and then climbed from the car, hitting the remote door locks. He then headed up to his front door just as his phone woke up, ringing inside his right hand. He saw that it was Brandi on the other line calling him back, and he almost decided not to answer the phone call from her.

"Yeah, Brandi?" Boss said as he was unlocking his front door.

"Oh, so you wasn't gonna call me back?" she asked with an attitude.

"For what?" Boss asked as he was locking the front door. "I tell you what though, Brandi. You was right about me being a man and telling you straight up what was real. So I'ma say this and be done with it and you!"

"Wait!" Brandi cried. "What you mean done with it and me?"

"I actually was feeling you, shorty, but all I was asking was for us to slow down so I could build myself. But after how you showed me how much you was down for me or respected me when you hung up the phone in my face, I think it's best I let you do you and I'ma do me! We cool though, shorty?"

"Oh, so that's how you wanna handle it, ReSean?"

"You decided this when you ended the call earlier. I don't do girls, ma! I'm into women, even if I'm younger!" Boss told her, before he hung up the phone on her.

# FOURTEEN

**BOSS PAUSED HIS XBOX** game system while playing Call of Duty after hearing the doorbell ring throughout the house. He walked out of his game room to the front of the house and to the front door. He looked out the peep hole and saw Vanity standing on the other side of his door. He unlocked and opened the door for her to come inside.

"Hey, babe!" Vanity happily cried, kissing Boss's lips before entering the house and looking around. "This is nice, Boss. This where you live, huh?"

"Pretty much!" Boss answered while locking the front door behind him. "What happened with the detective?"

"From how everything went, everything is good," Vanity explained to Boss.

She then followed him into the back bedroom that had an oil-shined round table and four cushioned fold-out chairs. She sat down beside him on the couch that was positioned in front of the 36" flat-screen TV.

"I got his number! He gave me his card," Vanity informed.

"You took Gina back to the hotel?" Boss asked as he began playing his game again.

"Yes!" Vanity answered. "But I was talking to her, and she wanted me to ask you if you could take her to see her husband."

"Alright! But do me a favor though, shorty."

"What is it, boo?"

"Take Gina shopping and get her some things and get her hair taken care of also."

"I'll take care of it tomorrow," Vanity promised.

She then reached for her purse and opened it. She pulled out a chrome gun and handed it to Boss.

"This is the gun I got for you. Is it okay?"

Boss paused the game again when he recognized the chrome .40 caliber Ruger. He took the banger from her hand, only for Vanity to then pull out a box of bullets, which she also handed over to him.

"This is definitely good, shorty. You looked out for real, ma," Boss said as he looked the piece over.

Vanity smiled at the surprising kiss Boss had just planted on her. She sat staring at him a few moments before she spoke: "Babe, you feel like going out with me tonight?"

"Where are we going?" Boss asked while loading the magazine of the Ruger.

"You told me you wanted me to leave Pink Palace, so I got a new spot at this club out in Miami Beach called Club Climax. The owner is a friend of mine, and she wants me to come by the club tonight to see how everything is running."

"What time are we leaving?" Boss asked, cocking the Ruger and then ejecting the magazine again, only to replace the bullet that was now in the chamber of the .40 caliber.

\* \* \*

"Malcolm!"

Malcolm looked up from his phone and read the text message from Pink Palace's owner. He was caught off guard and sat staring in surprise when he noticed his personal bodyguard, Moses, and his step-sister standing in the doorway of his den.

"Destiny, what the hell are you doing here?" he asked her as he stood up from his seat after tossing his phone onto the coffee table.

"Malcolm Sr. sent me out here," Destiny told her step-brother as she entered the den. "It seems you're having a problem out here in Miami, and he sent me here to help solve the problem."

"When have I ever needed help solving a problem, Destiny?" Malcolm questioned her as he dropped back down into the sofa. "And let's just keep it real: Malcolm Sr. sent you out here to watch me."

"I just told you I'm here to help," Destiny told Malcolm as she bent down and picked up her step-brother's phone. After noticing the incoming text message, she opened the message and began reading: "Who's Pleasure, Malcolm?"

Malcolm opened his eyes and lifted his head from the back of the sofa to see his step-sister with his cell phone. Malcolm hopped up from his sofa and snatched his phone from Destiny's hand.

"Don't fuck with my shit, Destiny!"

"Are you going to answer my question, Malcolm?" she asked him, ignoring his attitude.

"She's nobody!" Malcolm answered as he once again dropped back down into the sofa.

"So is that why you're asking questions about what club she's going to, Malcolm?" Destiny asked her step-brother.

"What do you want, Destiny? Why are you in my house?" Malcolm asked loudly after a deep sigh.

"Because I don't want to be here, and until we find out what the problem is out here in Miami, I have to be here. So how about filling me in on what's really been happening down here?"

* * *

Boss pulled up in front of Vanity's apartment complex. He drove through the front gate and headed toward her building near the back of the complex. Boss called Vanity's phone to let her know he was outside.

"Hello."

"What's up, shorty? You ready?"

"I just finished fixing my hair. You here yet?"

"I'm outside, ma."

"I'm coming now, babe."

After hanging up the phone and dropping the cell phone in his lap, he parked the Ferrari in the middle of the parking lot. Boss then pulled up the rolled blunt from the center console along with his lighter and lit the blunt. While he was taking a deep pull from it, his phone went off in his lap. Boss looked down and saw the blocked name and number. He started to ignore the number, but instead decided to answer it.

"Yeah?"

Boss listened to the automatic recording asking if he would accept a collect call. He then broke out in a smile, hearing his best friend who was like a brother to him. Boss laughed when he heard his boy's government name, and quickly accepted the call.

"What's good, big bruh?" Trigger yelled excitedly once the call was processed.

"What's good, De'Neair Stanley?" Boss laughed.

"Oh! So, you gonna clown me now, huh?" Trigger said, laughing lightly after Boss cried out his whole government name.

Boss was still laughing when the passenger door opened. He looked to his right as Vanity climbed inside the car and leaned over kissing him.

"Real talk though, lil' bruh. What's good with you?" Boss said into the phone.

"Everything, everything!" Trigger replied. "Murphy got word to me that you was looking for me, and he gave me this number. He says you sounded like you was doing big things in Miami."

"I'm on my boss shit, lil' bruh!" he told his boy. "You already know you got a place on my side of the table, fam! Ain't no question about that!"

"That's love, my nigga!"

"How long you got left though?"

"Three weeks, fam!"

"Alright. I'ma have something for you when you jump. I hope you're still handling your business though."

"What's my name, nigga?" Trigger asked. "Ain't shit change, big bruh, but the body count!"

"That's what's up!" Boss said, smiling and happy to be talking to his boy.

Boss continued his phone call with Trigger until the time ran out and the phone hung up on them. Boss then dropped the phone back in his lap.

"Babe, who was that?" Vanity asked.

"My brother!" Boss answered with a smile. "He's getting out of jail in three weeks, and we're going up to pick him up and bring him back with us to Miami."

"So, I'm going with you to Atlanta?"

"I'ma need my lady to hold me down!" Boss told Vanity. "You got me, shorty?"

"You shouldn't have to ask me that, Boss!" Vanity told him.

She then took the blunt and lighter from Boss and re-lit it.

"But this is the second time you've called me your lady. Is that what I am, Boss?" she wanted to know.

"You shouldn't have to ask me that, shorty!" Boss answered, throwing Vanity's words back at her.

Boss then winked and smiled at her, and she smiled back. She then leaned over and kissed him.

# FIFTEEN

**TRIGGER FINALLY WALKED OUT** of Atlanta's main jail, along with three other inmates, after finishing out the rest of his jail sentence. Trigger quickly broke off from the others and walked out onto the side. He heard a homeboy from his unit call out to him as he began walking out toward the street.

"Hey, yo, lil' bruh!" a familiar voice yelled out.

Trigger looked back over his right shoulder and instantly recognized the dude walking toward him from across the street. The young man was dressed in dark black jeans, a white T-shirt, a black blazer leather jacket, and a white and black fitted Yankees cap. Trigger broke out in a smile as the guy got closer.

"My muthafucking brother!"

Trigger threw his arms around Boss, who gripped him in a tight embrace. Trigger held his only true friend and brother, even if they didn't share the same blood. He broke their embrace after a moment with tears running down his face.

"Come on, lil' bruh!" Boss said, dropping his arms across Trigger's shoulder as the two of them started back across the street. "You hungry, playboy?"

"Hell yeah!" Trigger yelled, causing Boss to burst out laughing. Trigger shook his head and smiled, and then asked, "How long you been out here?"

"Long enough!" Boss answered as he stopped beside a white and lime-green colored Suzuki motorcycle.

"Yo!" Trigger cried all hyped up after instantly recognizing the Suzuki GSX–R1000R sports bike.

He then looked over at the shadow-gray Ducati SuperSport S sports bike.

"Big bruh, who's shit is these?"

"They ours!" Boss answered as he tossed Trigger the key to the Suzuki. "That's your bike, lil' bruh! I know you like them shits! Let's go eat, and then I wanna introduce you to some people."

Trigger was still smiling when he picked up the bike helmet and then climbed on. He started up the Suzuki and then pushed down the dark-tinted helmet shield, just as Boss rode past him on his Ducati. Trigger pulled off behind Boss and felt the power from the Suzuki. He then slowed to a stop at the corner after Boss took off and made a left turn. He gave the bike some gas, pulled out, and picked up speed, hearing the strength from the engine.

* * *

Vanity heard knocking at the room door as she was walking out of the bathroom. She started toward the front of the suite, only to hear her cell phone begin to ring. She quickly answered the door and saw that it was Eazy standing there. She then rushed back across the suite to pick up her phone on the bed.

"Hello!" she answered.

"Where you at, Vanity?" Malcolm asked her.

"What do you want?" Vanity asked, looking over at Eazy, who was on his phone texting someone. "Why are you even calling me? I've told you I'm seeing someone."

"Vanity, we need to talk."

"We have nothing to talk about, Malcolm!"

"Who the fuck is you yelling at?" Malcolm yelled back. "I don't know what's up with you, but whoever this nigga is, you—!"

"You don't want no problems with my man, Malcolm! I'm

telling you one last time. Don't call me, and leave me the fuck alone!"

Vanity hung up the phone on him and slammed it down onto the mattress. She looked over at Eazy, who had something to say.

"You told Boss about this nigga Malcolm stressing you?"

Vanity shook her head.

"I don't want Boss and Malcolm getting into it, Eazy. I know how Malcolm can be, but I've seen that other side of Boss, and I can only see bad shit coming out of all of it!"

"Let me ask you something, Vanity. You know how both Malcolm and Boss are, but who's your man?"

"You know Boss is my babe."

"So your loyalty is to Boss or Malcolm?"

"What type of question is that?" Vanity asked in anger. "You know my loyalty is fully to Boss."

"Alright. So why keep your man in the blind? Put my nigga on point then!"

Vanity heard her room door unlocking. When she looked up, she saw Boss walking inside. She broke into a smile and walked over to him from the bed and gave him a kiss.

"God damn!" Trigger said in disbelief as he stared at the five-foot-four, 34D-25-42, thick-as-hell and fine-as-hell female who was all over Boss.

Boss smiled after ending the kiss with Vanity and seeing the look on Trigger's face. "Trigger, this is my girl, Vanity, and the homeboy against the wall over there is my nigga Eazy!" Boss introduced.

"So, this is the trigger-happy Trigger!" Eazy stated as he and Trigger dapped up. "Boss told me a lot about you, my nigga."

"He told me about you too, playboy," Trigger replied. "My brother also told me about you, but he ain't tell me you was this fine, shorty! Please tell me you got a sister or a friend that looks exactly like you," Trigger said as he turned and looked at Vanity.

"Sorry!" Vanity told him with a smile. "But you're cute, and I may have a friend who would like you. I'll introduce you to her when we get back to Miami."

"That's what's up!" Trigger replied, still smiling.

"Yo, Boss!" Eazy spoke up, grabbing his attention. "Bruh, we have a problem back in Miami!"

"What's good," Boss asked, losing his smile.

"Rico just hit me up a few minutes ago. Word is that Travis White is in town and just had a sit-down with all the names in Miami. But both Malcolm and Travis White are supposedly working together to find out who killed Victor White and who's behind the blue devils."

"Whoa! Wait up!" Trigger spoke up. "Who the fuck is Travis White and Malcolm, and I heard another name too. Victor something?"

"White!" Boss finished for Trigger, but then he said, "I'll explain what's up after we meet back up with Murphy to pick up this work."

"You ready to go, babe?" Vanity asked Boss.

"Yeah! Grab our bags, shorty!" Boss told her.

Boss then walked over to his black leather backpack that sat on top of the round table on the far right side of the room. He went inside the bag and pulled out two semi-automatic Glock .19s, and then walked back over to Trigger and handed him the two bangers.

"I figure you'll love these, lil' bruh. They're yours!"

Trigger smiled as he took both Glocks and looked over both pieces. "This is what the fuck I'm talking about!" Trigger said.

\* \* \*

"I'm coming!" Brandi heard from inside the apartment.

She stood outside of Erica's apartment a few minutes, when the front door finally swung open.

"Brandi! Hey, girl!" Erica cried as she and Brandi hugged each other.

She allowed her friend inside the apartment and asked, "Where you been at? I called you and got your voice message."

"I left and went back to Oakland to see my mom and sister for a little while," Brandi told her as the two of them walked into the front room and sat down.

"You seen ReSean?" Erica asked. "Brandi, Boss and Eazy left town on business, girl. They should be back probably late tonight or tomorrow morning." Erica sighed softly.

"Did he change his number? I tried calling him a few times, and it said his phone wasn't in service."

"Brandi!" Erica said, getting up and moving over to sit beside her friend. "Boss changed his number because Vanity wanted him to."

"Vanity wanted him to?" Brandi asked, with her face balled up in anger. "Why the hell does ReSean care what . . . what! ReSean's with Vanity now, Erica?"

"Brandi, you—!"

"Just answer the question, Erica!"

"Vanity is Boss's girlfriend, and she even lives with him now!" Erica admitted with a loud sigh.

"I knew his lying ass wanted that bitch!" Brandi spit

angrily. "All that shit he told me was a lie!"

"Brandi, come on!" Erica begged. "You basically pushed Boss away! All he asked—!"

"You taking his side now?" Brandi asked in a nasty tone. "You've only known his ass a little over a month and a half, and you're taking his side over mine?"

"Brandi, it's not about taking sides, and you know it! Boss tried to talk to you, and you hung up on him. He told me what happened between you two. But while you was acting stupid, Vanity was showing him that he was important to her, and she was willing to give him whatever he wanted. In return, he gave her what she wanted. Himself!"

"I see you're a fan not only of ReSean now, but of that bitch Vanity too!" Brandi told Erica as she stood up from her seat. "It's fine though! Since ReSean wants to be nasty, I can be nasty too! Just let him know that I got something for his ass!"

"Brandi!" Erica cried out to her friend as Brandi stormed off.

Erica stood up from her seat just as Brandi was snatching open the front door and slamming it shut behind her, leaving the apartment.

Erica dropped back down into the couch with a heavy-sounding sigh. She sat there a few minutes thinking before she got up, headed to her bedroom, and grabbed her cell phone to call Eazy.

* * *

Boss made the drive back from Atlanta and headed to Miami. He rode with Vanity inside the Toyota Highlander that he rented for the trip to Georgia. He shifted his eyes over to his right mirror and looked back at Eazy and Trigger driving the new Chevy Silverado 1500 Z71 crew cab truck that he had bought for Trigger. Eazy and Trigger were transporting the Ducati and Suzuki bikes back to Miami in it.

"Babe, what's on your mind?" Vanity asked, after closely watching Boss the last ten minutes.

Boss turned his head and looked over at Vanity, just as she looked over to him.

"I'm just thinking, shorty. I'm good though!" he finally replied.

"You thinking about your mother again?"

"Not really! I was thinking about the work we got in here with us, and also about this shit with Travis White and Malcolm's ass!"

"You think there's going to be trouble?"

"I'm guessing there may!" Boss answered, just as his phone woke up. When he pulled out his iPhone, he saw Eazy was calling. "Yeah!"

"Bruh! Erica just hit me up, and she says Brandi came by looking for you. But get this! Erica said she told Brandi about you and Vanity, and Brandi tripped out, my nigga! She sent out a message."

"I'm listening."

"She says since you wanna be nasty, she'll be nasty too, my nigga! Supposedly she got something for you, or something like that."

"Got something for me, huh?" Boss repeated. "I'll deal with that once we get back to Miami."

Boss hung up with Eazy and slid his phone back inside its case on his waist. He then looked over at Vanity.

"What happens now, Boss?" she asked.

"Mother—!" Boss started, but thought about his answer and then admitted, "Brandi sent me a message. She found out about us and said she had something for me!"

"That bitch better go ahead about her business before she gets her ass beat!" Vanity stated, upset just by the thought of Brandi.

# SIXTEEN

**BRANDI GROWLED IN AGGRAVATION** after being awakened by the sound of her doorbell, after feeling like she had just gone to sleep. She looked over at her bedside clock and saw that it was only 4:27 a.m. She heard the doorbell ring again, so she angrily threw off her blanket and climbed from the bed.

Brandi put on her silk housecoat, walked out of her bedroom, and headed down the stairs as the doorbell rang again. She yelled that she was coming. Once she got to the front door and got on her toes to look out the peephole, she quickly ran her hand through her hair and opened up her housecoat, allowing her boy shorts and bra set to show. She then unlocked and snatched open the front door.

"What the hell are you doing here, ReSean? What do you want?"

"We need to talk!" he told her as he walked straight into the condo past Brandi, who stood staring at him like he was crazy.

"ReSean, let me tell you something, boy!" Brandi yelled as she shut the front door and turned around to see him walking into her kitchen and opening her refrigerator. She stormed in after him, slammed the refrigerator door, and yelled, "Nigga, who the fuck do you think you is just walking up in my shit and going up in my shit? I ain't that bitch Vanity, nigga!"

"Believe me, shorty. I'm well aware!" Boss told her, seeing the quick shocked expression that shot across her face. He continued before Brandi could say anything else. "I'ma say this one time, Brandi. We did our thing, but you made the decision to end things, so I'll say this and leave. Stay away from me, Vanity, and my people! You send another threat at me, and my next visit won't be to talk to you! We clear?"

"Nigga! You don't scare me!" Brandi yelled, grabbing Boss's arm as he started to walk away, only to snatch him back to face her. "I ain't Lucky and the rest of those people I know you killed! You better watch how you talk to me before people find out that it's really your ass that's pushing those blue devils out around the city, and got all these real gangsters like Malcolm and Travis White looking for you while you're hiding out like a bitch with your soft ass! Get the fuck outta my house, nigga, before I call the cops!"

Boss controlled his anger and simply smirked while nodding his head. "Remember what just came outta your mouth, shorty! I want you to say it again the next time we're face to face!" Boss said.

"Get the fuck out!" she yelled, watching Boss leave her condo.

She rushed to the front door and snatched it open after he walked out. Brandi stood at her door and watched as Boss opened the driver's door to his Ferrari and climbed inside. She noticed for the first time that the bitch Vanity was inside the passenger seat and was staring straight at her.

"No this muthafucker didn't bring this bitch to my house!" Brandi fumed, completely pissed off that Boss had disrespected her.

She stood watching him drive off and decided then and there she was calling Malcolm and telling him everything she knew about Boss.

* * *

"Boss, what happened?" Vanity asked him as they drove

away from Brandi's house.

Boss remained quiet for a moment and then simply said, "We have to move outta the house!"

"What?" Vanity cried out. Why?"

"Brandi's on some other shit, and I don't trust her. So we're moving today. Call that shorty you know at the Coconut Creek area and tell her we changed our mind about that townhouse we saw."

"I thought you didn't wanna move that far out?" Vanity said while digging out her phone to do as Boss had asked her.

"I changed my mind!" Boss replied while also pulling out his own cell phone.

\* \* \*

"Yeah," Malcolm answered half asleep, only waking from the sound of his ringing phone. He looked over at his clock and saw that it was 4:45 a.m.

"Malcolm, it's Brandi. I need to tell you something."

"Who?"

"Brandi! You and I met some time back at Pink Palace. I go by the name Privilege."

"Yeah! I remember you now. The short, sexy, light-skinned chick," Malcolm told her after remembering. "What's up though, baby girl?"

"I got some information I know you would love to have."

"What's that?"

"I know who's behind the blue devils that have been having everybody tripping and going crazy. But I also know who's behind the murder of the guys you've been hearing about."

Malcolm sat up in bed after what he was just told. "Look,

Privilege. Brandi. Whatever your name was again, I'm not with game playing, so if you're not 100 percent sure about this shit you're telling me you know, don't say shit else and just hang up the phone now!"

"How about this?" Brandi stated. "What if I told you Vanity cut you off because she's messing with the same guy who's taking over the city?"

"Bitch, ain't nobody taking over my city!" Malcolm barked at Brandi.

Brandi smiled, knowing that her words affected Malcolm, just as she had hoped they would. "So, do you want to know who this person is or not?" Brandi asked.

\* \* \*

Malcolm hung up with the stripper Privilege after she told him where to meet in half an hour. He then called Travis White, ignoring the aggravated tone he received from calling so early. Malcolm told him what he was just told and explained what the plan was. He then hung up with the drug lord and called his step-father, Malcolm Sr. Malcolm hung up and called his step-sister after only getting his father's voice mail.

"Hello!"

"Destiny, this is Malcolm."

"I know, Malcolm. I can read your name. What do you know?"

"I just got some information about who's responsible for all this bullshit going on! I tried to call father, but I only got his voice mail."

"That's because Malcolm Sr.'s off dealing with a new business deal, Malcolm!" Destiny told her step-brother. "Look!

I'm on my way over to your place now, so we can deal with this together."

\* \* \*

"Big bruh, you sure about this shit?" Trigger asked Boss as he, Boss, and the rest of the crew were loading up Trigger's Chevy and Eazy's new GMC Denali Yukon with Boss and Vanity's things as they worked fast to empty out the rental house.

"Trigger, I see where you're going here, lil' bruh," Boss told his boy as he put the boxes he was carrying inside the back of the Yukon. "I ain't with all the hiding and running either, but I also gotta think about where I lay my head at night. Because I ain't the only one who lays there anymore, lil' bruh. I also gotta think about Vanity!" Boss said as he turned back and faced Trigger.

"I feel that, but just tell me one thing."

"What's up?"

"Once we got this whole moving thing finished and you're right about what you're thinking, are we gonna get at these muthafuckers who are responsible?"

"That's not even a question!" Boss answered his boy just as Vanity called out to him. Boss looked back toward the front door to see Vanity and Erica heading his way. He turned to face her as she stopped in front of him holding up his phone. "Who's this?"

"It's the detective I spoke with that day with Gina," Vanity told Boss. "He wants to talk to you."

"Talk to me?" Boss asked with a confused look on his face. "How the fuck does he even know me?"

Boss watched as Vanity shrugged her shoulders. He then shook his head and after a brief moment put the phone up to his ear.

"Yeah! Who's this?"

"Good morning, Boss. I'll make this quick. Word on the street is that you have someone that's informing both Malcolm Warren and Travis White about your whereabouts, but that's not why I'm calling you. I figure we could talk and I could inform you of something much more important to you and your well-being."

"I'm listening."

"Not over the phone. In person."

"You're not serious, right?" Boss chuckled.

"I'm very serious. I'm offering you my help."

"And I'm supposed to trust and believe you, right?"

"I tell you what. We meet, and if what I have to say isn't worth my life, you can let your friend you just picked up from Atlanta—Trigger, is what they call him?—have at me. He can do what he's known for doing! What do you say, Boss?"

Boss shifted his eyes over at Trigger as their eyes met. He then looked over at Vanity and the others, who all stood around watching and waiting on him to finish on the phone. Boss decided to take a chance and gave the detective the address to the new townhouse where he, Vanity, and Trigger were moving.

"Babe, why did you just give him our new address?" Vanity asked Boss as soon as he hung up the phone.

"Because he's got information he says is very important that I want to know," Boss told her before turning toward Trigger. "And if dude's not on the right page, my lil' brother is gonna erase his ass from the storyline."

"Now that's what the fuck I'm talking about!" Trigger said, with a devilish-looking smile on his face.

\* \* \*

Malcolm rode inside the back of Travis White's Bentley Flying Spur along with Travis White and Destiny while following behind two Range Rovers full of Travis White's gunmen. A third Range Rover followed behind the Bentley. Malcolm sat quietly and was staring out the window while both his step-sister and Travis were talking together.

Malcolm heard the ringing of a phone. He looked over at both Destiny and Travis, only to see his step-sister pulling out her cell phone. Malcolm turned his focus back out the window. Destiny called out to him as he looked back over at her.

"Yeah?"

"It's Malcolm!" Destiny told him, handing her step-brother the phone.

Malcolm took the phone from Destiny, sighed a bit, and then placed the phone to his ear. "Yeah, Pops!"

"What was you calling me for?"

"Why didn't you just call my phone instead of calling Destiny's phone?"

"What do you want, boy?"

Malcolm shook his head and sighed again. He then began telling his father everything he learned over the last few hours and what was about to happen in the next five minutes. He also told him what was agreed upon between him and Travis White.

"Who is this woman who's giving you this information, Malcolm?" his father asked his son once he finished speaking.

"That's not important."

"Who is she?" Malcolm Sr. barked, cutting off his son.

"She's a dancer at the club, Pops," Malcolm told his father.

Malcolm stopped talking when he heard Travis announce their arrival. Malcolm then focused on their surroundings and noticed the front entrance of a gated community.

"Pops, we're here now! Let me call you back!"

"Stay on the phone!" Malcolm Sr. told his son. "Let me know what's going on!"

Malcolm sighed and decided not to argue with his father as he focused out his window after the Bentley drove through the gate and once again began following the two Range Rovers in front of them.

"Nice neighborhood this Boss lives in!" Destiny stated, looking around at the really nice houses. "He has good taste!"

"I must agree!" Travis said while also looking around.

Once the Bentley stopped in front of a house that looked surprisingly big, Destiny made a comment about wondering how much money Boss was really seeing from the sale of the blue devils. The three of them then sat watching Travis White's men rush inside the house. Malcolm sat in his seat giving his father a play-by-play of what he was able to see.

"Here we go!" Travis announced, after seeing his men exit the house.

However, he then noticed his lieutenant, Howard, step out of the house and look directly at the Bentley and shake his head.

"What the hell just happened?" Malcolm asked, watching Travis's man Howard walk out to the Bentley.

"Explain why you're out of that house with nothing to show me?" Travis demanded after letting down his widow to speak with his lieutenant.

"Mr. White, the house is empty," Howard told his boss. "There's nothing inside the house."

"Sir!"

Howard looked to his right as one of his men walked up beside him and handed him a cell phone. "Who's this?" Howard asked his man after taking the phone.

"The phone was ringing inside the house in the kitchen," one of the security guards told Howard.

After nodding to his men, Howard placed the phone up to his ear. "Who's this?"

"Who this is isn't important. This is for Malcolm, so if you're not him, then give the phone to him."

Howard looked over at Malcolm sitting in the car. He handed him the phone through the window. "It's for you, Mr. Warren."

"For me?" Malcolm asked, taking the phone from Howard while passing back Destiny's phone. "Hello," he began after placing the phone to his ear.

"Malcolm?"

"Yeah! Who's this?"

"Listen. I'm going to say this once, playboy! Don't look for something you really don't want to find. Go on with doing you, and I'll do me. But if we have to have this conversation again, I can promise you things won't end the same as they do now. Also, tell your boy Travis White to go home. Let it go, and go home before it's too late. First and last warning for the both of you!"

Malcolm kept the phone to his ear until the line died. He then lowered the phone.

"Who was that?" Travis asked.

"I'm pretty sure that was just the guy we were here to see,"

Malcolm told the drug lord as what he was just told played back out through his head again.

* * *

"So, what do you think?" Detective Aaron Wright asked, once Boss hung up the phone after talking with Malcolm Warren Jr. "You still think I'm not to be trusted, or have I earned at least a little breathing room?"

Boss stared at the slightly heavyset, clean-shaven, brown-skinned detective. He then nodded toward Trigger, who began lowering one of his two Glocks.

"Alright, detective. Talk!"

"May I sit now?" Wright asked, to which he received a nod from Boss.

They sat out on the back patio of the new townhouse in which they were moving. The detective then continued once he was seated on a cushioned fold-out chair.

"As I said earlier while on the phone, I'm offering my services to you and your organization."

"How much?" Boss asked, just as he heard the sliding glass door open. He looked to his left to see Vanity exit the house.

She walked over to him and kissed him before stepping between his legs and sitting down between them. "What's going on?" she inquired.

"The detective here was just about to tell us how much he wants for his services," Boss told Vanity while staring at Detective Wright.

"How does $3,000 sound to you?" Wright asked while holding Boss's stare.

"That's $36,000 a year!" Boss stated, doing some quick

math.

"Hold on, babe," Vanity spoke up, before addressing the detective herself. "Boss told me you had something important to tell us. If we decide to deal with you or not depends on what you have to tell my man and how important it is."

"Don't look at me," Boss told the detective. "She stated the demands, not me."

"Okay!" Detective Wright stated, with a smile. "I'm sure we all remember the case over in Opa-locka. Well, you all slipped and left one person alive: Daniel Cook. He was Brandon Cook's younger brother. He's still alive and has agreed to testify against all of you at the house that day he was shot and his brother was killed."

"Where is he?" Boss asked.

"He's being watched at Jackson Hospital. But I may be able to get one of you inside to take care of what was started," Wright told Boss.

Boss nodded his head after listening to what the detective had just told him. He didn't need to say anything since Vanity spoke up: "We will send you this week's payment by wire transfer, detective."

Wright nodded his head in agreement and stood up from his chair.

"You have my number. Call me no matter the time or the reason," the detective informed them.

"How can you get one of us into the hospital room?" Boss asked him.

"I can get a police uniform that one of you can dress in that will allow you to enter Daniel Cook's room," Wright explained.

"Trigger!" Boss called out.

"I'm already on it, big bruh," Trigger spoke up as he motioned the detective back into the townhouse.

Once both Detective Wright and Trigger went back inside with the others, Vanity looked back at Boss and noticed the expression on his face. "What's wrong, babe?"

"Thinking!"

"About what now?"

"How to deal with Brandi."

"What do you mean?" Vanity asked with an attitude. "Boss, she just tried to have you killed all because she's jealous! What's to think about?"

"So, you think I should just kill her too, huh?" Boss asked, with a shake of the head.

"Wait a minute, Boss!" Vanity said as she stood up from his lap to stare down at him. "This bitch just tried to have you killed but you still got feelings for this ho?"

"Vanity, relax!"

"No! Fuck that, Boss!"

"Vanity!" Boss said, grabbing her hand, only to have her snatch it away from him.

"Don't touch me! You need to make your mind up who you want to be with, nigga! That bitch cares nothing for you, because if she did, she wouldn't be trying to get someone to kill you. I know one thing though. I won't stay with a man I can't have 100 percent!"

Boss watched Vanity angrily storm off and go back inside the townhouse. He stayed where he was but turned his attention out toward the ocean view. He sat re-thinking and reviewing all the plans he put together for himself, including what Vanity had to say.

# SEVENTEEN

**VANITY HEARD THE BATHROOM** door when it opened, even over the intercom that was playing Mary J. Blige's "I Can Love You." She heard the music being lowered just as the lights were dimmed a moment afterward. She knew who it was even before the glass shower door opened behind her.

"You still made at me, ma?" Boss asked as he wrapped his arms around Vanity from the back.

The two of them stood under the water that was cascading down on them from the wide showerhead.

Boss kissed her neck and then whispered into her ear: "Shorty, you know where my heart is. You got it already."

Vanity lay back against Boss and let out a sigh. "Boss, I love you," she said as she kissed his neck.

"You love me, huh?" he asked playfully. "How much do you love your man, shorty?"

"Enough to hold him down through whatever!" she told Boss.

Shutting her eyes, Boss's gentle hands began running over her body and up to her breasts, where he began playing with her overly sensitive nipples.

"ReSean!"

"Oh, now I'm ReSean, huh?" Boss said.

He continued playing with Vanity's right nipple while he moved his left hand down between her legs, working on her already wet pussy. He played with her lips the way she liked them to be played with.

"You gonna cum for your man, ma?"

"Yesssss!" Vanity moaned as she reached back and began stroking Boss's dick, only to step forward out of his arms and bend forward a little.

She looked back at him and smiled a mischievous grin. "Give your baby some of her dick!"

"This what you want, huh?" Boss asked, smirking as he stepped in behind her and readjusted the shower head to rain down on top of both of them.

He then positioned his manhood at Vanity's opening, only to have her reach back and take hold of his dick again and begin running the head up and down between the lips of her pussy.

"Push it in!" Vanity told him, once she had the head positioned at her opening.

She closed her eyes slowly as Boss slid inside of her. "Oh God. Yesss!"

\* \* \*

Boss got Vanity through three orgasms, with her screaming through each one while in different positions. Boss exploded a load that felt big as hell, and he was now lying beside her in their new bed. Vanity picked out a new bed after throwing out the one Brandi had first bought for him.

"Babe! What am I gonna do about my job?" Vanity asked Boss, breaking the silence between the two of them.

"You mean because of the distance from Sample, Florida, back to Miami?" Boss asked as he played with a few strands of her hair.

"Boss, that's a long drive going back and forth each night, and then I'm driving way out to Miami Beach."

"Then why not open a club out this way and get this money out this way?" Boss told her as he threw off his blanket and climbed out of bed.

"Where you going?" Vanity asked, sitting up inside their bed watching him.

"Smoke!" he answered, grabbing a sack of weed and both his Ruger and a blunt wrap. "You coming?"

Vanity climbed out of the bed and put on one of Boss's T-shirts and then followed her man from their bedroom to the front of the five-bedroom, seven-and-a-half-bath townhouse. She held onto Boss's waist and leaned in against his side as her man led the way out onto the back patio. Once they were seated in one of the chairs with Vanity in his lap, Boss lit up the blunt he rolled on the way outside.

"Babe, was you serious about the whole opening a club out here thing?" Vanity asked.

"You want to?" he asked as he blew thick weed smoke to his left, away from her face.

"It does sound like a good idea."

"Then we're doing it!" Boss replied, seeing the bright smile that broke out on Vanity's face. Boss looked over his right shoulder when he heard someone driving up.

"It's Trigger!" Vanity stated as they sat watching the Chevy 1500 park in front of the townhouse behind Boss's Porsche. She paused a moment when a uniformed police officer climbed from the truck.

"Relax!" Boss told her, feeling Vanity's body stiffen. "It's Trigger dressed up."

"What's up, family?" Trigger called out seeing both Boss and Vanity.

He walked around to the far side of the townhouse.

"Hey, Trigger!" Vanity said, smiling at him as she took the blunt Boss handed her.

"Hey, big sis!" Trigger called her before looking over at

Boss. "That's taken care of, big bruh."

Boss nodded his head in response and said, "You ready to put in some more work?"

"Always," Trigger answered with a smile. "Who's it this time?"

"You remember the shorty I told you about?" Boss reminded him.

"You mean that Brandi shorty, big bruh?" Trigger asked, seeing Boss nod his head in answer. "When you want it done?"

"Make it soon, lil' bruh," Boss suggested, watching Vanity's reaction out of the corner of his eye.

* * *

Once they were back in bed and Vanity was asleep with her head on his chest, Boss lay staring at the ceiling while playing with Vanity's hair. He was thinking, so he reached over to his bedside dresser, picked up his phone, and pulled up a phone number and called it.

"Hello!" April answered after three rings.

"April, this is Boss. You busy?"

"Not really. I'm just getting home from a business party. What can I do for you though?"

"How soon can you get me 2,500 of those?"

"Boss, come on! I'm a pharmacologist! Do you know what that is?"

"You work with creating the stuff I'm paying you for, along with other stuff."

"I'm impressed!" April said. "We've discussed my price. I can have you the 25 by tomorrow afternoon."

"Call me when you're ready and I'll set the place and time

for the meeting."

"I'll be in touch."

Boss tossed the phone back onto the table. He then rolled over and faced Vanity, wrapped his arms around her as she snuggled in close to him, and kissed the top of her head while closing his eyes.

\* \* \*

"Babe! Babe, wake up!" Vanity cried, shaking Boss awake after being woken by his loudly ringing cell phone.

She shook him again until he answered her.

"Yeah, what's up, baby?"

"Boss, it's Eazy. There's a problem," Vanity told him as she handed him the phone.

"Eazy, what's up?" Boss answered.

"Bruh, we got a problem. The spot out on 135th Street in Opa-locka is on fire!"

"What?" Boss yelled, shooting up in the bed. "Fuck do you mean it's on fire?"

"I got a call from the lil' dude next door to Gina's old house, and he told me that the spot is on fire. I'm heading over there now with Rico and Magic."

"I'm on my way now," Boss yelled, hanging up the phone while at the same time jumping out of bed.

"Babe, what happened?" Vanity cried as she sat up in bed and watched Boss get dressed, throwing on a pair of dark grey cotton sweatpants.

Boss explained to her what was just told to him as he stepped into his white and gray Air Max. He didn't worry about a jacket or a shirt, but he grabbed his Ruger and his keys, and headed for the door, when Vanity yelled his name to get his attention.

"Babe, what about Trigger? I want him with you," she told Boss, feeling calmer, for some reason, at the thought of Trigger being with Boss.

"Wake him up, Vanity. Tell him what I just told you, and tell him to meet me at the spot out in Opa-locka," Boss told her as he took off out of the room.

Boss paused once he was outside the front door, after noticing that his Porsche was blocked in by Trigger's truck. He then jogged over to the garage and opened it, only to see that his Ferrari was blocked in by their motorcycles. "Fuck it!"

Three minutes later, Boss was shooting away from the townhouse and jumping onto I-95. Five minutes later, he was opening up the Ducati on the expressway, ignoring the biting wind that was ripping at his upper body.

Boss made it to Miami in less time than it took to get to Coconut Creek, jumping off the I-95 and speeding to Opa-locka. He swung his Ducati down the street where the trap spot was located, and came across a crowd of people, firefighters, and police officers. He slowed down his bike until he stopped a few feet from the crowd. He stared at the house that was black from the fire that the firemen were still putting out.

"Boss!"

Boss heard his name and looked to his right to see Eazy, Rico, and Magic heading his way. He pulled off his helmet as his boys walked up. "What the fuck happened?"

"This shit was intentional!" Eazy told Boss. "My lil' dude said these dudes showed up and set fire to the spot."

"He see any faces?" Boss asked.

"He said there were about four guys wearing all black, but

he did get a glimpse of a light-skinned guy inside of a white Bentley who spoke with one of the guys," Eazy explained.

"Where's he at now?" Boss questioned.

"Magic, go get lil' nigga Lloyd," Eazy told him.

"What's up, my nigga? What you thinking?" Eazy turned and asked Boss.

"I'm about to see how true my thoughts are!" Boss stated, seeing Eazy and a young and slightly heavy-looking kid walking back over.

"Lloyd, this my nigga Boss," Eazy introduced the young kid.

"I know who he is," Lloyd told Eazy as he nodded to Boss.

"What's good, lil' homie?" Boss started, but paused when he caught the sound of a motorcycle.

He turned around to see Trigger's bike swinging down the street. He sat watching as his friend pulled up smoothly beside him.

"What's the deal, big bruh?" Trigger asked once he pulled off his helmet and looked straight at Boss.

"We about to find out now," Boss replied as he looked back toward the kid.

"Tell me something, youngin'. What did the guy inside the Bentley look like?" Boss asked Lloyd.

"I saw him from the front window at my dad's house, but I saw a scar down the left side of his face, big homie."

"Could you point him out if you saw him again?" Boss asked the kid.

"Hell yeah!" Lloyd answered.

"Eazy, let me see your phone," Boss told him, taking the cell phone Eazy pulled out. He then called up a number that he had programmed.

"Detective Wright here!"

"It's Boss. You busy?"

"Hold on a moment."

Boss waited a moment and stared back over at the house. He then focused back on the call when the detective came back on the line.

"Boss!"

"Yeah!"

"Okay, what's up?"

"I need a favor. Can you pull up a photo of Travis White?"

"It may take a while, but I probably can."

"Call this number back once you get it."

"Will do."

After hanging up with Detective Wright, Boss looked back at Lloyd and asked, "Youngin', you wanna get something to eat?"

\* \* \*

Boss sat inside a Wendy's that was just a few minutes away from the trap house. He was murdering a double stack with Lloyd and Trigger while Eazy, Rico, and Magic stood outside the restaurant smoking and talking. Eazy's cell phone finally went off, and Boss looked down at the screen to see the blocked name and number. Boss then picked up the phone from the table and answered it. "Yeah!"

"Boss, it's Wright."

"You got that?"

"I just got it. I'll send you a picture to your phone."

"I'll hit you back if I need you," Boss told him before hanging up the phone.

"What did he say?" Trigger asked as he stuffed his mouth full of fries.

"I'm waiting on a picture of—" Boss began, just as his phone vibrated in his hand. He looked down at the incoming text and saw an image appear. He then slid over his phone to Lloyd. "That's who you saw, youngin'?" Boss asked.

Lloyd put down his sandwich, wiped off his hands, picked up the phone, and then looked at the picture. "Hell yeah! This is the dude right here, big homie!"

"You sure?" Boss asked him.

"Look at his face!" Lloyd told Boss while handing him the phone. "Look at the left cheek. You see the scar?"

Boss did notice the scar Lloyd mentioned. He gave a nod in agreement and instantly called Detective Wright back.

"Detective Wright," he answered at the start of the second ring.

"I need information where—"

"I already got an address for Travis," Wright cut off Boss. "I heard a few minutes ago about the fire and figured that's why you wanted a picture of Travis. I'll send you the address now."

"Good job," Boss stated after hanging up the phone.

Boss stood up out of his seat, followed by Trigger, who did the same.

"Youngin', it's time to bounce. We got business to handle, but I owe you!"

* * *

"Come in!" Travis White called out after hearing the knock on his penthouse suite door.

He looked back over his shoulder from where he stood in front of the opened sliding glass door where he was smoking a cigar.

"Mr. White," Howard said as he entered the suite and saw his boss at the door.

"You're here, so does that mean this person has been taken care of?" Travis asked, turning back and facing the balcony.

"You was right, Mr. White!" Howard told his boss. "This guy Boss showed up. He is a young boy, but he has four other guys with him. We kept a watch on him, but, sir, we somehow lost him."

"Lost him?" Travis asked in a calm voice, even though he felt otherwise. "You just told me that there were four other guys with him, Howard. How can you lose five men?"

"Sir, two were riding motorcycles while the other three rode in an SUV. Once the two motorcycles split up from the SUV, we lost them. This Boss guy was on one of the bikes," Howard explained, just as his cell phone went off. "What is it?"

"I gave you a warning and you didn't listen."

"What?" Howard yelled into the phone. "Who the fuck is this?"

"Tell your boss that since he was looking for me, I'll find him. It'll be just a few minutes."

When the call ended, Howard looked at the screen. "Sir, I'll be right back," he said after looking over toward his boss.

"Is there a problem?" Travis asked, turning to face his head of security.

"No, sir. I just wanted to check on a few things, sir," Howard told his boss while backing toward the door.

After Howard left the suite, Travis turned back to his cigar and continued smoking. He then began wondering who the hell the young man was who was proving to be a bigger problem than he should be. "Howard, I want this bastard found and brought to me! Are we understood?" Travis called out, when he heard the door open behind him.

"Am I the bastard you're looking for?"

Travis heard an unfamiliar voice and turned around, only to freeze as his eyes took in the sight before him. He was unable to believe exactly what he was seeing.

"You was looking for me, right?" Boss asked as Trigger shoved Howard down to the floor onto his ass.

He looked down at Howard and then back to a frightened and staring Travis, who was trying to hide his fear but wasn't doing a very good job.

"I gave you a warning for you to leave, and had you listened, we would never have had to meet!" Boss began.

"Son of a b—!" Travis started, but quickly stopped in the middle of what he was saying.

The second young man who had held Howard at gunpoint snatched out a twin model of his gun and was now pointing it directly at Travis.

"I bet you're wishing you would have taken my warning and left Miami, huh?"

"Okay, listen," Travis said, getting control of himself. He straightened his clothes and then continued, "We're both businessmen. We can work out something. How much is it going to take? I've got money, or do you want drugs? I have all you could ever want. Just name it and it's yours!"

Boss chuckled as he stood up and stared at the supposed kingpin, who was actually weak and a straight bitch. Boss laughed as an idea came to him. "Alright. This is what I'm going to offer you. If you accept it, I won't kill you, but if you refuse, then you'll be meeting Jesus real shortly!" Boss explained.

"I'm listening," Travis told Boss in a calmer tone, thinking he had things under control now.

"I want $500,000 wired to an account within the next two hours," Boss told him, watching as a shocked expression crossed the drug lord's face before he regained composure once again.

"So, where am I sending it?" Travis asked in agreement of the deal that was just offered to him.

Boss pulled out Eazy's phone and called Vanity.

"Hello!"

"It's me!"

"Babe, is everything okay? Did Trigger find you?"

"He's with me. I need you to listen right now though. Give me your bank account information, and I want you to call me back once you see that money was wired into your account. You understand?"

"Okay, babe."

After getting Vanity's information, Boss hung up and tossed the phone over to Travis. "Make the call," Boss told him.

* * *

After hanging up with Boss, Vanity sat in bed waiting for an update to her bank account balance. She waited and waited, until she had to use the bathroom. After using the toilet, she returned to the bedroom and checked her laptop. She saw no difference in her account. She then walked out to the kitchen in the huge townhouse and set down the laptop on the marble countertop. She walked over to the refrigerator to find something to eat, since she was suddenly hungry.

After ten minutes, Vanity finished cooking a late-night breakfast for herself, so she sat down at the counter next to her laptop with her plate. She looked at the account balance again, and still saw there was no difference. She just shook her head and then began eating her food. Vanity heard the house phone ring, so she stood up and walked over to the cordless phone on the wall to answer it.

"Hello!"

"Vanity, it's Erica. You speak to Boss yet?"

"He just called a little while ago," Vanity informed her as she sat down to finish eating. "He just asked me to do something. What's wrong?"

"Eazy just called me. Rico got shot, and they're on their way to the hospital. I tried calling Boss, but he's not answering his phone."

"He didn't take it, Erica, but I have his number that he told me to call him back at. Let me call you back afterward."

After hanging up with Erica, Vanity called Boss at the number he provided her, and she recognized it as Eazy's cell phone number. She only waited for half of a ring, when Boss answered.

"Yeah!"

"Boss, we got a problem, babe. Rico got shot, and they're on their way to the hospital now."

"What happened?"

"I don't know yet. I just called to tell you what's happening. I gotta call Erica back."

"Alright! I want you to call me back once you know where they're at, and I'll be there in a little while. What about your account? Any difference?"

She looked back at her computer screen again and saw nothing different in her balance. "Babe, it's still the same!" she replied to Boss.

"Alright. Hit me back."

After hanging up the phone, Vanity called Erica back to find out where they were taking Rico.

\* \* \*

Boss stared at Travis the entire time he was on the phone with his lady. He then slid the phone into his pocket and pulled out his Ruger, which caused Travis's eyes to grow wide in fear.

"It seems that nothing's happened, and time's run out!" he told the drug lord.

"Wait! I swear I had the money wired to the account you gave me," Travis told Boss. "It just takes time!"

"I'm out of time!" Boss told him. "I'm needed someplace else, which means you're out of time also."

"Wait!"

*Boom! Boom!*

*Brrrrrrr! Brrrrrrr!*

Boss looked over at Travis White's body after putting two bullets in him. He then saw Howard's face half missing from Trigger's semi-automatic.

"Fun over. We gotta go!" Boss said to a smirking Trigger.

# EIGHTEEN

**BOSS WAS NOTIFIED THAT** Rico and the others were at Parkway Hospital. He and Trigger walked into the waiting room and found Vanity already there. Detective Wright was there as well taking down notes on what supposedly had happened. Boss was filled in that a six-man hit team went after Eazy, Rico, and Magic after they had dropped Lloyd back at his house.

Boss spoke with Detective Wright for a few minutes, filling him in on the two bodies back at the Hilton Hotel where Travis was staying. He also explained that the bodies were probably still not found because Travis had rented out the entire top floor of the hotel. Boss then rejoined his people after Wright left, with the promise of calling him later once everything was worked out.

"Boss, what happened, babe?" Vanity asked as he entered the waiting room.

"Everything's going to be good, shorty!" Boss told her as he sat down beside her. He then dropped his arms across her shoulders and looked at Eazy, with Erica meeting his boy's eyes. "Lloyd's good, right?"

"Yeah," Eazy answered. "Lil' homie got inside the house before anything jumped off."

"How bad was Rico hit?"

"I ain't sure really. There was a lot of blood though!" Eazy replied. "What's up with the thing you and Trigger went to handle?"

"Let's just say he won't be making that trip back home after all!" Boss replied, just as everyone turned and saw a tall brown-skinned male doctor enter the waiting room.

The doctor informed everyone that Rico was no longer in real danger. He had taken a bullet in his upper left arm and had a bullet rip across the side of his neck, cutting his skin deep but not deep enough to be fatal.

"Can we see him?" Eazy asked the doctor.

"You can. But I ask that you all please not stay long," he told the group, before exiting the waiting room.

The gang stood up and all left the waiting room together to find Rico's hospital room, with Eazy in the lead. Once they found the room number, they all walked in and saw Rico laid up but still smiling.

"What's up, y'all?" Rico said, still smiling as his people crowded around the bed.

"What's good, gangster?" Boss said, with a small smile. "We heard how you saved Magic's life by snatching the boy out of the way from them shots."

"I couldn't let my nigga get hit!" Rico said, smiling as he and Magic touched fists.

He looked back to Boss and asked, "What I wanna know though is what happened with the thing you and Trigger went to handle earlier?"

"He'll never have to wonder what life after death is like no more!" Trigger stated, earning him a smile from each of his boys.

"How long you have to be here, Rico?" Erica asked him.

"I can leave tomorrow," Rico replied. "I'ma call my lady and have her come pick me up then."

"I want you to hit me up once you get outta here. I wanna talk to everybody," Boss stated, looking from Rico to each of his boys' faces.

Boss chilled at the hospital with Rico a little while longer before the nurse asked them to let Rico rest. The boys all said their goodbyes and left. Once outside and in front of the hospital, Boss and Vanity said goodbye to Eazy, Erica, and Magic while Trigger stood off to the side talking with a cute red-skinned nurse he saw as they were leaving.

Boss pulled Vanity off to the side after Eazy and the others walked off. He looked over to Trigger and the nurse, and then back at Vanity.

"Shorty, you think the homeboy you know with the guns can get something bigger?" Boss asked her.

"I can ask him."

"Alright. Hit dude up and let him know your man is looking to get something that spits more than one shell with a pull of the trigger!"

"I'll take care of it later today."

"What's up, family?" Trigger asked as he walked up on Boss and Vanity. "We ready to go?"

"You done running game?" Vanity asked him playfully.

"For now!" Trigger answered with a smile. "I wouldn't have to though if my big sis would hurry up and introduce me to this friend she told me about!"

"Boy, come on!" Vanity cried, smiling as she wrapped her arms around his waist as the three of them walked into the parking lot.

After exiting the hospital, Vanity drove her Corvette, with Boss and Trigger following her on their motorcycles. She smiled as she watched her man and his best friend playing and showing off on their bikes.

They made it back to Coconut Creek a short while later and pulled up to the townhouse. Vanity parked her car in the garage while Boss and Trigger parked their bikes out in front of the

J. L. ROSE

driveway. She climbed out from her car and heard Boss and Trigger laughing.

"You two ain't nothing but some grown-ass kids!"

"I got your kids!" Boss told her as he playfully slapped Vanity on the ass as they walked up to the front door.

Once the three of them were inside the townhouse, Trigger broke off and headed to his room while Boss headed to the kitchen for something to drink.

"Baby, I was thinking," Vanity began as she followed him into the kitchen. "We was talking about opening a club up here. Do you mind if I have my girl Gigi go looking around with me later today?"

"It's cool!" Boss told her. "I gotta meet this shorty April about these pills when she calls, and I also wanna go by and see Gina later."

"You still taking her to see her husband this weekend?" Vanity asked him as she grabbed her laptop. She froze when she glanced at the screen and said, "Oh my God!"

"What?" Boss asked, looking at Vanity, who had a concerned expression on her face.

"Boss!" Vanity cried, looking at her man. "Babe, what did you do?"

"What are you talking about?" Boss asked her, with a confused look on his face.

"This!" She told him as she turned her laptop around for him to see.

Boss walked over to the counter and looked closely at the screen. He slowly began to smile at the numbers he was seeing in Vanity's account.

"Ain't this a bitch! He actually did wire the money!"

"Who wired the money, Boss?" Vanity asked him.

"There's $500,000 in my account that wasn't there before!"

"Let's just say it's a gift for all the hard work I've been putting in!" Boss told her with a huge grin. "While you're out today, I need you to hire a new attorney and also open me a new bank account. Make that two accounts. Transfer and divide up $300,000 into the two accounts."

"What about the other $200,000?"

"Hold it!" Boss told her. "You may need it, or I may need you to handle something for me in the future."

Vanity shook her head at a still-smiling Boss. She then walked around the counter to him and wrapped her arms loosely around his neck.

"You are something else, ReSean Holmes, and I love you so much, boy!"

* * *

Malcolm groaned at the sound of his ringing cell phone, waking him out of his sleep. He rolled over and reached blindly for his phone, until his hand made contact. He then snatched it up and answered: "Who the hell is this?"

"Malcolm, it's Destiny. Turn on the TV!"

"What?"

"Turn on the TV to the news."

"Destiny, I'm sleeping!"

"It's Travis White, Malcolm!"

Malcolm opened his eyes after what he had just heard his step-sister say. He shot up out of bed and grabbed the remote. He turned on the wall unit and quickly found the morning news on channel 7.

"What the fuck!" he said to himself, seeing a picture of

Travis White on the television.

He listened as the news reporter stated that White's body had been found with two bullet shots to his face, along with thirty-three-year-old Harold Stoker, whose face was ripped away by what seemed to be some type of machine gun.

"Yeah, I'm still here!" Malcolm replied to Destiny yelling his name.

"Malcolm, this can't be that young boy Boss! Do you think he's behind this?" Destiny asked, sounding a little worried.

"Who else could it be, Destiny?" Malcolm asked her. "Nobody else in the city would have been crazy enough to try some shit like this! Travis White is as well-known as Pops is!"

"How the hell did Boss even get close enough to Travis White to do this?" Destiny questioned.

"That's something I'm still trying to figure out now!" Malcolm replied. "Travis White had a strong security team, so I can't think of any way Boss could get past them and inside the hotel, murder Travis, and then leave!"

"Malcolm Sr. is going to go crazy once he finds out about this!" Destiny told her step-brother. "My question to you, though, is what are you going to do now?"

"Truthfully, Destiny, I really don't know what I'm going to do right now!" Malcolm responded.

* * *

Boss got in a few hours of sleep before Eazy called and said he and the others were on their way over to the townhouse. Boss was still in the shower when Vanity appeared, sticking her head inside the shower to let him know she was leaving with her best friend, Gigi, who was out front waiting for her.

166

After Vanity left and he finished his shower, Boss dressed in a pair of blue, yellow, and light green blended color Polo jeans; a wifebeater; and a pair of all-white Air Max. He then picked up his white-on-white fitted Yankees cap, just as his cell phone began ringing. He walked over to the bedside dresser and picked it up.

"Yeah!"

"We outside, bruh," Eazy told Boss.

"Come on in," Boss told him as he picked up his Ruger from the dresser.

After hanging up with Eazy, Boss left the bedroom and walked toward the front of the house. He then heard a knock on the door and voices as Trigger had let all the other guys inside the house.

"What's up, my nigga?" Rico said, smiling with his arm in a sling.

"How you feeling, playboy?" Boss asked him as he embraced Eazy and then dapped up with Magic and then Rico.

"I'm good," Rico answered as the five of them walked into the den to sit down.

Once everyone was seated, Trigger lit up a blunt while Boss picked up the Newports from the marble and glass coffee table. He then began what he had to say to the group.

"Alright, fellas. We're about to make some changes on how we run business. I was trying to keep things quiet and let us get this cash without too much trouble, but this ain't the type of city you can hustle in and stay too quiet. This is what we about to do though. I want each of you to get at every soldier you know who's ready to make this money but ain't got a problem putting in work. We're about to take over this city, and everybody that fucks with me is about to eat as much as they want, and any muthafuckin' body in the way can definitely get it! It's either get the fuck down or get laid the fuck out! Period!"

"Now this is what the fuck I'm talking about!" Trigger added once Boss paused a brief moment and handed the blunt over to his right to Eazy. "I also want each of you to relocate out of the city. No one's to live in the city while we're working. We also need to find a new spot to trap at!"

"I already found a new spot," Magic spoke up, cutting off Boss. "I got this homeboy that has a spot over in Brown Sub. He's pushing a little weed. I'ma holla at him and see if he's trying to get some paper with the team!"

"Get on that!" Boss told Magic, but then looked over to Trigger and said, "You handling what I told you about Brandi, right?"

"As soon as we done here, I'm gone!" Trigger responded.

"You good, lil' bruh. Go ahead and handle that!" Boss requested.

Boss then watched as his boy stood up and left the den.

He then turned back to Eazy, Rico, and Magic and said, "I got Vanity handling something for me with getting us some war weapons. So when shit turns up, it'll be us turning it up!"

Boss continued discussing different business matters and agreeing on different plans. He ended the meeting when April called and asked where their meeting was. After the others all left to go handle their business, Boss put on an azure Polo shirt and then grabbed a white leather blazer that had azure stitching inside. On the back of the jacket was a lion wearing a crown on its head.

Boss left the house through the kitchen door that led into the garage. He hit the remote to his Ferrari and unlocked the doors. He then walked up to the wall and hit the button to open the garage door, before he climbed into his ride. Boss started up the engine and then let down the top. He left the engine running and jogged back to the door and back into the house to grab the black tote pouch that was for April, and then he ran back to the car. After he pulled out of the garage, he hit the remote to close the garage as he drove off.

\* \* \*

April saw the beautiful convertible Ferrari and then recognized the extremely handsome young man who went by the name of Boss. She sat watching the car turn into the parking lot of the Burger King where they were meeting. April climbed out of her Audi RS7 and locked the doors behind her. She crossed the parking lot and entered the fast food restaurant, and then walked around to stand in the four-person line to order food.

April looked up at the menu board, but she could smell Boss's cologne once he was standing close enough behind her.

"You smell delicious, Boss!" she said in a lowered voice.

"You still looking good!" Boss replied, seeing the change in April's expression from the side of her face, letting him know she was smiling.

"Is everything okay?" he asked.

"I'm here, aren't I, handsome?" she responded as she got closer to the front of the line.

As planned, April handed her keys to him behind her. She felt his hands while he took them from her before he left and disappeared.

April made it to the counter and placed a simple order. After paying for her meal, she exited through the same door through which she arrived. She walked over to her car and opened the driver-side door. She was not surprised that the door was already unlocked and the keys were in the ignition. She leaned over and set down her food in the passenger seat, and then reached beneath her seat and felt something.

April smiled when she saw the pouch. She first glanced around and then opened it. She smiled even wider when she saw the money inside. She then closed it back up and pulled out her cell phone and called Boss's number.

"Yeah!" Boss answered in the middle of the first ring.

"Is everything okay?" she asked while still smiling.

"Everything's good, shorty. I got the two backpacks from the trunk."

"Call me when you're ready again or whenever you want something else I've got to offer only you, handsome!"

"Bye, April."

April heard his sexy-sounding laugh before he hung up the phone, and she shook her head.

"Damn! That man is too damn sexy! I would love to have a taste of some of him!"

* * *

Boss picked up Gina after handling his business with April. He first took her out to lunch at Collins Smokehouse, the new restaurant for which he was a silent partner. There, he and Gina had lunch for free.

"How is my sweetheart?" Evelyn asked as she walked up to Boss and Gina's table and hugged Boss and kissed his cheek.

"Hi, momma!" Boss said with a smile, before introducing Gina as his friend.

"I know who Gina is," Evelyn said, smiling as she hugged the younger woman. "How is it you know my son, Gina?"

"ReSean has been helping me get myself together." Gina answered, smiling affectionately at Boss. She then looked back toward Evelyn and asked, "So, when did you and Mr. Collins open this business, Mrs. Collins?"

"Almost two months ago!" Evelyn answered, only for Boss to speak up again. "Momma, are you hiring?"

"Why I know you're not looking for a job!" Evelyn told him jokingly.

"Gina needs a job!" Boss stated, nodding over to a smiling Gina.

"You looking for a job, Gina, sweety?" Evelyn asked her.

"Yes, ma'am. Are you hiring?" she asked.

"We are now!" Evelyn told her. "If you're finished eating, you can come with me now, and we can take care of your paperwork."

"I'll be here!" Boss told Gina when she looked at him with a questioning expression.

Boss watched as Gina and Evelyn walked off together. He shook his head and pulled out his phone to call Eazy, but then heard someone behind him.

"Hey, gorgeous. You want some company?"

Boss looked back over his shoulder, even though he recognized the voice. He then stood up as Vanity smiled at him and gave him a hug, then kissed him.

"What you doing out here?" he asked.

"Gigi wanted to try the new smokehouse," Vanity told Boss, nodding over to her best friend, who sat across the restaurant smiling and staring at the two of them.

"What are you doing here? I see two plates, so who are you

with?" she looked back and asked Boss.

"Gina," Boss replied. "How'd everything go with looking for a building for the club?"

"We've found two spots, but I like this one place that's really nice."

"And?"

"And what, Boss?"

"Vanity! Come on, shorty. I pay attention to you, and I know when you're not telling me everything. So talk!"

"The place is really nice, Boss, and it's in an open space that sits on four acres. But the building is an old warehouse." Vanity smiled.

"How big is it?"

"It's two stories, a little over eighteen thousand square feet."

Boss chuckled after hearing what Vanity had to tell him. He then sat back in his seat and folded his arms across his chest.

"How much, shorty?"

"I was thinking we could lease the building to see how business will be at first, boo."

"How much, Vanity?"

"It's $25,000 a month, ReSean."

"You've already spoken with the leasing agent, haven't you?" Boss said, nodding his head.

Vanity nodded her head back at him and reached over for Boss's hand. Once he gave her his hand, she kissed the back of it.

"Babe, please! I really want this building, and you told me I could have what I wanted," Vanity replied.

"Did you handle what I asked you to take care for me?" Boss asked her, changing the subject and noticing the change in Vanity's expression.

She sighed loudly as she released Boss's hand and sat back in her seat.

"I called him, and he said he would call me back once he got some stuff together," she answered him.

"Call me when he calls you," Boss told her, just as Gina showed up.

"Hey, Vanity!" Gina cried out happily. She hugged her and then looked over at Boss and said, "ReSean, thank you so much. I can start work tomorrow."

"Well, we need to get you a car then," Boss added as he stood up. "You ready to go?"

"Sure!" Gina answered and then waved goodbye to Vanity.

Boss turned to follow Gina, but looked back at a staring Vanity and said, "Yeah! Go ahead and get the building, ma! I'll see it with you later."

A huge smile broke out over Vanity's face. As she watched her man walk out of the restaurant, she could see that most of the other women inside had turned to stare at Boss's fine self exiting as well.

Once outside and walking across the parking lot, Boss's cell phone went off. He hit the locks by remote and then pulled out his iPhone and saw that Trigger was on the line.

"What's good, Stanley?"

"Yo, Boss! She's gone, big bruh."

"Whoa! What you talking about?"

"The shorty you told me to go see about," Trigger explained. "She never came home, and when I looked inside the spot, it was empty, playboy. She bounced!"

"Shit!" Boss said as he took a deep breath. "Alright. Do me a favor, lil' bruh. Vanity's in the city, and until she leaves, I need you to watch out for her."

"Where's she at?"

"She's up here at Collins Smokehouse."

"I'm on my way."

"Hit me up after Vanity leaves the city."

"I got you, big bruh!"

After hanging up with Trigger and reaching for the gear shift, Boss looked over at Gina, after she called out his name.

"Yeah, what's up, Gina?"

"You love her, don't you?" Gina asked him. "Vanity, I mean. You're in love with her, aren't you?"

"Why you ask me that?"

"Because, do you remember when I told you how King used to act with me about my protection? I just sat here and listened to the same thing King would have said about me to one of his boys."

"Yeah! I love her," Boss admitted and smiled at Gina's words.

"I know," Gina replied with a grin.

Boss backed the Ferrari out of the parking lot and then started toward the exit.

## NINETEEN

**DESTINY LEFT HER STEP**-brother's mini-mansion after having a long talk with him about everything that was going on in the city with the mysterious Boss. She then dug out her ringing phone from her Dolce & Gabbana purse, only to see her step-father was calling.

"Yes, Malcolm," she answered the phone.

"Why haven't you reported to me on what's going on there, Destiny?"

"Malcolm, I've been dealing with—!"

"Why did I have to find out what happened to Travis White?" Malcolm Sr. demanded, cutting her off while she was talking. "Who the hell is behind what's happening in my city, Destiny? Do I need to make a trip out there?"

"I'll handle it, Malcolm."

"Handle it then!"

After hearing Malcolm Sr. hang up the phone after yelling demands at her, Destiny tossed her phone over onto the passenger seat. She slowed her Porsche Macan Turbo, turned the SUV into a BP gas station, and pulled up in front of an open pump. She shut off the engine and climbed from the Porsche after snatching both her purse and phone from the seat. She then hit the locks and slammed the car door before walking around the SUV and in the direction of the gas station.

Once she was inside, Destiny picked up a bottle of raspberry iced tea and then headed for the front counter. She froze when the door opened as she stared as the most gorgeous and sexy guy she had ever seen before walked inside. She tore her eyes away from him as he walked past her, but not before catching his greenish-golden eyes.

"Damn!" Destiny said to herself, before asking for twenty dollars in gas for her Porsche and paying for her tea.

She first smelled his cologne and then saw him walk up behind her as she was turning to leave.

"Hey!" the guy spoke up, nodding to Destiny.

"H-Hi!" she barely got out as she once again tore her eyes away from him as she left the store.

Once Destiny returned to her Porsche and began pumping her gas, she couldn't help but stare at the Ferrari that was parked at the pump behind hers. She looked back toward the gas station entrance just as the door opened and the guy stepped outside. She slowly looked him over, loving his whole style, even though he was dressed simply with a fitted cap.

"What's your name?" she heard herself ask, even surprising herself, since she was acting out of her normal self.

"What's up, shorty?" the guy asked as he stopped next to her to start pumping his gas.

"I asked your name," Destiny told him. "Are you going to answer my question or not?"

Boss smirked at shorty's sassy attitude. He then looked at her slim but nicely curvy build. She was five foot five, 140 pounds, and had a 34C-28-42 frame. She was dressed in a Dolce & Gabbana outfit that hugged her body perfectly and showed that she was not only from money but that she even carried herself like she was from money.

"You plan on answering my question, or are you just going to stand there and look at me?" Destiny asked while looking him over as well.

"It's Boss!" he answered, and caught her surprised expression that appeared on her face one moment, but was gone in a second.

"Boss, you say, huh?" Destiny asked, unable to believe her luck of actually standing face to face with the infamous Boss.

Even her own step-brother was in fear of him, but he would never admit. She finished pumping her gas and then walked over beside him. "So, Boss. Where'd you get a name like that?"

"You plan on telling me your name, or am I supposed to guess it?" Boss responded.

"It's Destiny. But you can call me your woman!" she told him. She then held up her cell phone and asked, "What's your number, husband?"

"Unavailable," Boss replied.

"Why?" Destiny asked, lifting her light golden-brown eyes to meet his.

"I'm already taken, shorty," Boss admitted as he returned the gas pump.

"You're taken is what you're telling me, right?" Destiny stated, remembering the Vanity woman Boss was supposedly seeing. "I'm new in Miami, and you're the first person I've spoken to that's worth my time, and truthfully, I think you're gorgeous. So, what do you say, handsome?"

"Where you from, smooth talker?" Boss asked her, smiling at the game she was trying to spit at him.

"I'm from New Orleans," Destiny admitted. "So, are you going to let me take you out, handsome?"

Boss stared at shorty for a few moments and then gave her his phone number.

"Gimme a call a little later on today."

"Trust me, I will!" Destiny told him, smiling as she turned away and walked back to her car.

Once inside her Porsche, Destiny looked in her rear-view mirror back at the Ferrari, only to see that Boss was inside. She smiled as she dialed Malcolm's number and listened to the phone ring as she started up her SUV.

"Yeah, Destiny!" Malcolm answered after two rings.

"Where are you?"

"About to handle business with a few people. Why?"

"Because you're not going to believe who I just got finished talking to."

"Destiny, I don't have time—!"

"Boss!" Destiny said, cutting him off. "I just met and spoke with Boss."

"What? Where at? How does he look?"

"Relax, Malcolm," she told her step-brother while still smiling. "I have his cell number, but I have plans for this Mr. Boss."

"Destiny, just tell me where this guy's at? I'll deal with it."

"Malcolm, you tried this your way already. Now I'm going to show you how to deal with Boss. You're either with me or not. Which is it going to be?"

Destiny listened to her step-brother angrily going off, and laughed once he gave in to her demands.

* * *

Boss pulled up in front of Lloyd's father's house a short while later, after leaving the gas station. He parked in front of the front yard and shut off the engine. He then climbed from the car and glanced around before shutting the car door and walking into the yard.

Boss knocked on the front door and waited. When no one came to the door, he knocked again. He heard the door unlock, and a moment later he started to smile when he saw Lloyd. But he quickly balled up his face when he saw that the boy had a black eye and a busted lip.

"Who did it, lil' homie?"

"My dad," Lloyd answered truthfully as he lowered his head.

"Where the hell is he at now?" Boss asked, looking the young boy over and seeing the condition he was in.

"He works at the automotive shop up the street from here," Lloyd told Boss, still staring down at the ground.

"Come on!" Boss told him. "You're coming with me! Fuck this spot here!"

Boss led Lloyd from the house and out to his Ferrari. He climbed back behind the wheel, and a moment later he was pulling off speeding up the block. He made it to the automotive shop in less than five minutes.

"Which one's your pops?" Boss asked as he and Lloyd sat in front of the shop staring at the four shop mechanics.

"The one with the long johns under his work shirt," Lloyd told Boss.

Lloyd stared at his father and then back toward Boss after hearing the car door open. Boss then climbed out, and after slamming the door, he walked around the front end of the car and straight into the shop's garage entrance. Boss crossed the garage and walked straight over to the guy who Lloyd pointed out as his father. Boss stopped beside him while he was talking. As soon as the man looked away, Boss swung and knocked Lloyd's father to the ground.

"What the fuck!"

Boss snatched his Ruger and swung it toward the guy with whom Lloyd's father was talking. Boss then cut off the homeboy who was about to defend the man who now lay on the ground with a busted nose. Boss shifted his eyes back to Lloyd's father once the defender backed up with both hands in the air.

"You like beating up your son, huh? Gimme one reason why I shouldn't end your sorry-ass life right now!"

"W-what are you talking about?" Paul asked while staring up at the young man standing over him with a gun. "I don't even know you, man!"

"Just know that I'm a close friend of your son, but because of your son, you're still breathing!" Boss told the father. "Don't worry about no more though. I got my lil' homie from now on!"

Boss turned and walked away from the father, leaving him on his ass in front of his co-workers and staring at him. Boss slid his banger back into his jeans as he continued toward his Ferrari and around to the driver's seat. Once he was back inside his car and pulled off a few moments later, Boss glanced over to Lloyd and saw that the young boy was staring down at his hands.

"What's up, youngin'? You wanna go back home, or you wanna come with me?"

"I don't wanna go back home. My dad's gonna do the same thing to me you just did to him," Lloyd said after looking over at Boss.

"Well, I guess that means you're coming with me then, youngin'!" Boss told the boy, hating the look on Lloyd's face since it reminded him of past days in his own life.

\* \* \*

Once back at Malcolm's place, Destiny broke down to her

step-brother her plans concerning Boss. She then called her step-father once she was back inside the Porsche, and left the mansion for the second time.

"Hello!"

"Malcolm, it's Destiny. I've got news for you."

"I'm listening."

"I've finally met with this Boss person."

"When?" Malcolm Sr. asked. "Is he taken care of yet?"

"That's why I'm calling, Malcolm," Destiny told him. "I've met and spoken with him, and this Boss isn't a stupid person. So just killing him won't be easy. I have a plan though."

"You have a plan, huh?" Malcolm Sr. repeated. "How is it that you're so sure that your plan will work when both Malcolm and Travis White both failed?"

"Because Boss doesn't know me, and I have one thing neither Malcolm nor Travis has—Boss's interest."

"I understand your plan now," Malcolm Sr. stated, fully understanding what his step-daughter was telling him. "Do what needs to be done, and keep me informed on what's going on."

After Destiny hung up with Malcolm Sr., a smile played across her lips. She then pulled up Boss's number.

"Yeah!" Boss answered in the middle of the third ring.

Destiny could hear music in the background of Boss's phone.

"Did I catch you at a bad time, handsome?" she asked, raising her voice.

"Who's this?"

"Excuse me?" Destiny cried out, actually surprised by this question. "You've actually forgotten me already, Boss?"

Boss remained quiet a moment and then spoke up, "Destiny, what's good, shorty? I'm kind of in the middle of something. What's up though?"

"I'm sorry to interrupt. I was only calling to see if you would like to go out with me tonight."

"Let me get back at you about that, alright? I'll call you."

When Destiny heard Boss end the call, she looked from the road to her phone and saw that the call had ended. She set the phone down on her lap and realized she had her work cut out for her.

## TWENTY

**BOSS TOOK LLOYD SHOPPING** and got the young boy all new clothes as well as things for school, since the two of them were in agreement that since Lloyd would be living with him, Vanity, and Trigger, Lloyd would be enrolled in school. Boss also spent time talking with the young boy and found out that he was sixteen and his birthday was in two weeks—the same day as his own. Boss also learned that the boy's mother no longer lived in the state. She had left Lloyd's father and moved away with some guy with whom she had been cheating on the father.

Boss heard his name and looked back over his right shoulder after both he and Lloyd left the Ralph Lauren store. Boss held up Lloyd, who saw Trigger jogging to catch up with them.

"What's good, big bruh?" Trigger said as he stopped in front of Boss.

With one arm embracing Trigger, Boss re-introduced Lloyd and then explained that Lloyd was coming to live with them now.

"I remember, lil' homie," Trigger stated as he dapped up with Lloyd, but then looked back to Boss. "Yo, big bruh. Your lady's at this huge-ass building, and after I told her I was coming over here to hook up with you, she wanted me to tell you to come through if you wasn't busy."

"You ready to go, or you still shopping, youngin'?" Boss asked Lloyd.

"I'm good, big homie," Lloyd answered, holding up both hands that were filled with more than four bags each.

"Let's get outta here then!" Boss said as the three of them

started toward the exit.

Once they were outside, Trigger broke off to head to his bike while Boss and Lloyd headed for his Ferrari. Boss then hit the locks as they approached the car, at the same time that his cell phone rang with a call from Eazy.

"What's good, playboy?" Boss said as he climbed into his car.

"Bruh, where you at?"

"Back on my end, why? What's good?"

"Both Magic and Rico just got back at me about what we discussed, and I just did a headcount of the niggas rolling with the team. With the sixteen I already got, we have a total count of thirty-eight."

"Wow, thirty-eight, huh?" Boss repeated. As he was leaving the parking lot, he spotted Trigger already waiting for him. "Eazy, check it. Gimme an hour and I'ma be back on that end. But make sure you let each of the thirty-eight guys know that if they're not really trying to get dirty, they shouldn't be there when I get there. Because I'm expect nothing but niggas ready to put in work to get this money. Period!"

"I got you, my nigga!" Eazy told Boss, before hanging up the phone.

Boss tossed his iPhone inside the center console after Eazy hung up. He then glanced over at Lloyd and saw the little man nodding his head to Rick Ross's "I Think She Likes Me" playing from the stereo. He turned up the music, which made Lloyd smile in return.

* * *

Boss followed Trigger from the mall for a twenty-minute

ride until they were pulling inside of a big parking lot with a huge two-story building. Boss parked his Ferrari next to Vanity's Stingray, but noticed the black Mercedes S63 parked on the opposite side of her car.

After Boss put up the top since Lloyd's bags were going to be inside, they climbed out and saw Trigger walking up beside them.

"How's it look inside?" Boss asked as they walked around the back end of the car where Lloyd stood waiting for them.

"It's big as hell, big bruh!" Trigger told Boss, smiling as the three of them left the parking lot and headed up the concrete steps to the four-glass-door entrance.

Once they walked inside the building and saw nothing but open space, Boss looked to his left and heard Vanity's voice as she called out to him from way across the room.

* * *

"That's my husband!" Vanity announced to the flirtatious leasing agent who introduced himself as Frank Frasire.

She and Gigi left the disappointed-looking agent and started toward Boss, Trigger, and a young boy. Once they met, Vanity threw her arms around Boss's neck and hugged him. She then slid her tongue into her man's mouth in a passion-filled kiss. She broke the kiss after a moment.

"I didn't think you were going to make it!" she announced.

"You wanted me here. I'm here!" Boss told Vanity as he nodded toward Gigi. "What's up, shorty?"

"Hi, Boss!" Gigi replied, surprised at how insanely good looking her girl's man was—even more so up close. "I'm Gigi. Vanity's best friend."

Boss nodded his head in response to Gigi, and then he leaned over and whispered something into Vanity's ear for a few minutes. Vanity then leaned back and looked into Boss's eyes and realized that he was serious about what he had just told her. She then looked over at the boy standing beside Boss.

"Hi, Lloyd. Boss told me you're going to be living with us now."

Vanity smiled at Lloyd's shyness. She then released Boss and stepped over to the young man and wrapped her arms around his shoulders. "Let's go see our new building Boss is letting me get!" she said to him.

Boss, Trigger, Lloyd, and Gigi followed Vanity over to meet Frank the leasing agent. Boss caught the look Vanity gave him when Frank began showing them the building.

"What do you think, babe?" Vanity asked Boss, a little bit after Frank began the tour of the building.

"This what you want?" Boss asked her as he looked around again.

"Yes, babe!" she replied as she wrapped her arms around his waist and leaned in against his side.

Boss nodded his head as he dropped his left arm across Vanity's shoulders. He then looked over at Frank.

"How soon can she get started fixing the place up?"

"I need to start with the—!"

"Here!" Boss stated, digging out a knot of money from his pocket and peeling off $500 and handing it to Frank. "Do whatever it is you gotta do to get my lady inside this building as soon as the last minute that just passed us. Are we understanding each other?"

"Clearly, sir!" Frank answered with a smile on his face while he pocketed the money.

\* \* \*

"Girl, I think I'm jealous!" Gigi told Vanity once the two of them were inside Vanity's Corvette following Boss's Ferrari out of the parking lot. "Boss is even sexier up close, Vanity! You say you met him on the Greyhound bus on the way home from Atlanta doing a party?"

"Yes, girl!" Vanity cried out smiling. "I almost lost my babe though to that bitch Privilege!"

"You mean Privilege who used to dance at Pink Palace?"

"Yeah. But what do you mean used to?"

"Girl, Privilege don't work at Palace no more. I just saw her two days ago leaving."

"Leaving to go where?"

"From what I heard, Privilege got herself into some shit and is leaving or already left town."

Vanity remained quiet a moment after hearing the news, and she was certainly going to talk to Boss about what she had just learned.

"So, Vanity!" Gigi spoke up. "What's up with Boss's younger brother?"

"Who?" Vanity asked, glancing over at her girl. "You talking about Trigger?"

"Yes, girl! His ass is cute. He got a girl?"

"Why don't you ask him?" Vanity told her girl, smiling at the thought of Gigi and Trigger together.

Once they made it to the townhouse and everyone was inside, Vanity and Boss allowed Lloyd to look through the house and pick out a room he wanted. But then Boss gave the young boy one rule, and that was to fully respect Vanity. He then left Vanity and Lloyd alone to meet up with Trigger.

Boss found his boy and Gigi together and peeped their vibe they were in. He then changed his route and headed into the kitchen to grab a Corona from the refrigerator, just as his cell phone went off.

"Boss, it's Wright. I've got that information you asked me to pull up for you," the detective explained. "I had to make you copies because the file isn't small."

"Alright. Meet me in a little while. I'll call you and let you know where I'm going to be at."

"I'll see you then."

After hanging up with Wright, Boss tossed the phone onto the countertop just as Vanity walked into the kitchen.

"You look tired," she told Boss as she walked up to him and wrapped her arms around his waist.

"I'll be alright," he replied. "How's lil' man doing?"

"He'll be alright," Vanity answered. "What happened to his face, Boss?"

"His pops beat 'im up!"

"Let me guess. You beat up his father because of it, didn't you?"

Boss smirked at Vanity, realizing how well she was beginning to know him. He then changed the subject.

"I gotta leave town in a few minutes, shorty. I gotta handle something with the fellas, but I'll try to get back before it gets too late."

"I won't expect you back too soon," she told Boss. "Just be careful and get back home, okay?"

"You got that, ma," Boss told her, kissing her forehead.

"Oh yeah!" Vanity said, remembering she had something to tell him. "I was talking to Gigi, and Brandi's name came up. From what Gigi told me, Brandi left town. I guess because her plans didn't work out how she hoped they would."

Boss nodded his head but didn't respond to what Vanity had just told him. Instead, he kissed her on her lips.

"Call me if you need me, or if you decide to come back into Miami."

"Yes, daddy!" Vanity playfully said, just as Trigger walked into the kitchen.

"What's up, big bruh? You ready to bounce?" Trigger asked Boss.

Vanity said her goodbyes to Boss and then kissed Trigger on the cheek. She followed them to the front door and then stood watching both her man and his best friend climb into Trigger's Chevy 1500.

"Girl, don't look all sad!" Gigi told her girl as she walked up beside Vanity. "That man will be back."

"I already know that!" Vanity told Gigi, even though she was in the middle of saying a silent prayer for both her man and Trigger.

* * *

Destiny sat on the sofa at her rented condo and was supposedly watching the news, but she was actually waiting for Boss's call. He had promised her that he would call her back after he finished up whatever the hell he was doing. Destiny then looked from the television to her cell phone that still sat silent beside her on the sofa, when it was supposed to be ringing off the hook with calls from Boss's ass.

"Who the hell does he think he is?" Destiny heard herself say while still staring at her phone.

She really had a problem believing Boss wasn't blowing up

her phone, when she was always used to ignoring different guys calling and trying to get her attention and a little bit of her time.

She snatched up the cell phone from the sofa before she realized what she was doing. She pulled up his number and called. She listened to the line ring one and then twice, only for the voice mail to pick up.

# TWENTY-ONE

**AFTER PARKING IN FRONT** of the new trap house out in Brown Sub, Trigger told Boss about earlier in the day. Trigger then hit the locks on the Chevy so he and Boss could climb out. Boss glanced around after shutting the passenger door and then walked around the front end of the truck. He wasn't surprised to see Trigger already gripping one of his Glocks, held down at his right thigh, and looking around the area.

"Come on!" Boss told Trigger as he led the way to the apartment, where they saw a group of three guys posted out in front of the apartment door.

"Whoa, my nigga!" one of the three guys said.

He quickly jerked back and reached for his strap, but froze since Trigger already had his Glock pointed at the homeboy while his backup was pointed at the two on the left.

"Who you niggas?" Boss asked calmly, looking from the guy to the others. "Where's Eazy, Rico, and Magic?"

"Who are you?" the homeboy who spoke first asked his question once again while watching Trigger but showing little fear.

Boss slowly nodded his head in approval and then said Trigger's name, which caused Trigger to lower both guns while still holding onto them.

"What's your name, playboy?" Boss asked the guy.

"Everybody calls me Butter!" Homeboy told Boss.

"Butter, huh?" Boss repeated. "Alright, Butter, I'm Boss, and this is my brother, Trigger."

"You Boss?" Butter asked with a look of disbelief on his face. "My fault, Boss. I ain't know, dawg!" Butter said after seeing Boss nod his head.

"Everything's good," Boss told him.

Boss then looked over at Trigger and nodded, which allowed Trigger to put away his burners. Boss then followed Butter and the other two guys out front into the apartment, where they saw more guys all piled inside the empty apartment, other than an old-looking sofa and some crates on which different guys were sitting. Other guys just leaned against the walls. Boss heard his name and looked to his left to see Eazy and Rico heading his way.

"What's up, my nigga?" Eazy said, first embracing Boss and then dapping up with Trigger. "We was starting to wonder when you niggas was gonna get here."

"Where's Magic at?" Boss asked, shifting his eyes and looking around the room that was a lot lower in volume.

Boss noticed a lot of the guys staring at him and talking in lowered voices to the guy beside them.

"Magic went to pick up three more guys that hit him up a few minutes ago," Eazy told Boss. "I let him hold my truck to put his niggas in."

Boss nodded his head but kept looking around the room. "Alright. Let's get this shit started," he said.

Boss stood in the center of the room while Eazy called for everyone's attention. Once the house was quiet and everyone was staring at Eazy, he introduced Boss to the house. He then nodded to Boss, before he and Trigger stepped off to the side. Everyone in the house looked at Boss, and Boss quietly stared around at every face that his eyes passed while looking around.

He then looked over to a light-skinned dude who said, "What's up, homeboy? You plan on saying something, or you getting off just looking at muthafuckers?"

"Relax!" Boss said out loud, stopping Trigger just as his

hair-trigger-tempered ass was about to start in the dude's direction.

He held homeboy's eyes even as Trigger stepped back beside Eazy and Rico, and then he spoke directly to the homeboy. "I'm really just waiting to see which one of you niggas isn't supposed to be among the group. I told my niggas I needed some real go-hard soldiers that was ready to take over this muthafucking city. You ready for this shit we about to get into, playboy?"

"That's what the fuck I'm here for!" homeboy replied, folding his arms across his chest while holding Boss's eyes.

"I hear that, playboy!" Boss stated. "Homeboy, tell me something. How many bodies you got?"

"Why don't you go check the morgue and get a body count!" he told Boss, causing a few guys to chuckle.

Boss smirked at homeboy's comment and asked, "What's your name, playboy?"

"I'm called Joker!" he answered, earning a smile from Boss.

"Alright, Joker," Boss said with a continued smile. "I'm sure Eazy, Rico, or Magic, whoever got you here, told you exactly why you all are here today, and since I'm not one for prolonged speeches, I want you all to listen real good. I'm asking each and every one of you now that if you're not really ready to catch a body or put in some work, there's the door. So leave now!"

Boss waited a few moments, and after no one left, he continued: "I've done my homework, and I know who's the power in this city. Malcolm Warren and Curtis Black. Black is powering the whole west side of the city giving him 25 percent. That gives Malcolm the other 75 percent in the north, south, and east. We're taking the full 100 percent of the city! Since Curtis Black has less power and we're still building, we're starting this takeover on his side of the city. There's only one rule, and that's you're either rolling with us or the city can dig a grave for the muthafuckers who are not with us!"

Bossed looked around after pausing a few moments to let what he just said soak in the heads of the guys around him.

"I'm going to set up three of you as my lieutenants along with Eazy, Rico, and Magic, but as of right now, I see only two I'm considering, and that's Butter and Joker. I haven't decided on a third yet!" Boss continued.

Boss was interrupted when the door to the apartment opened and in walked Magic. He was followed by a stocky-built dude with dreads that reached his wide shoulders. He was followed by a brown-skinned cute female who also had dreads that reached past her shoulders and brown tips. Boss showed loved to Magic by embracing him and then nodding to the big dude and female. He then turned back around to continue addressing the crowd.

"As I was saying, this city no longer belongs to Malcolm Warren or Curtis Black! We now own this city, even if we gotta raise the death toll and keep the streets painted red with muthafuckers' blood. Now as far as I'm concerned, this meeting is muthafucking over!" Boss ended.

Boss started for the door with Trigger right behind him. He then pulled out his vibrating phone and saw Detective Wright was calling, even though he thought it might be Destiny.

"Yeah."

"Boss, it's Wright!"

"Where you at?"

"I'm five minutes away from where you wanted to meet

at."

"You'll see the crowd once you get here. Just hit my phone back."

After hanging up the phone with the detective, Eazy, Rico, Magic, and the big man and the shorty with dreads walked up.

"Yo, Boss!" Magic started as he nodded to the big man and the female with the dreads. "This is my boy Savage and his sister, Black Widow."

"Savage and Black Widow, huh?" Boss repeated.

He looked over at the six foot three, 240-pound stocky, muscularly-built Savage, and then he looked at Black Widow, who was actually a lot prettier than he first thought. She had a banging ass, was five foot five and 137 pounds, and had a 34B-28-44 body that was easy to see even with her baggy clothes.

"Savage! Is there some meaning behind the name?"

Savage slowly smiled, which was just as evil a grin as Trigger's. He then answered in his deep voice that was low and sounded like a growl: "Just pay attention when I'm at work and you'll have your answer."

Boss nodded his head at Savage's answer and then looked back at Black Widow, who openly stared at him with a hint of what looked like interest in her eyes.

"You don't look like you should be out here in these streets, shorty. You cute! But then hearing the name Black Widow, I'm coming up with a few ideas that I'm sure are close to what you're probably capable of. And you're probably the deadliest one of all who's standing around here right now."

Black Widow smiled at what Boss was saying and took his comments as a compliment. She then looked over at Boss again with a growing look of sexual hunger.

"I think I've changed my mind about the pretty boy. I think

I'm going to really like him after all!" Black Widow called out to Magic.

"Boss!"

Boss turned when he heard his name and looked toward the street, where he saw a familiar Cadillac SRX. He then saw Butter and four other guys standing around the SUV and not allowing the driver to get out, even though he knew it was Detective Wright.

"Who's that, pretty boy?" Black Widow asked.

"It's business!" Boss stated as he walked off and headed out to the Cadillac. "It's cool!" Boss told Butter as he passed him, walking around the front of the SUV to the passenger side, and climbed inside.

"I see you've made friends," Detective Wright stated as Boss shut the passenger door behind him.

He ignored the detective's comments and then asked, "Where's this information you told me you got?"

Wright reached across Boss, opened the glove compartment, and removed a thick brown folder, which he tossed onto Boss's lap.

"Here are Malcolm Warren Sr.'s and Malcolm Warren Jr.'s records that you wanted to see."

"I didn't ask for his father's file," Boss stated while opening the folder and beginning to look through the papers.

"I figured since Malcolm Sr. started the business that his son is now running, you would want to know what you're up against once you actually try to go up against Malcolm Jr.," Detective Wright explained to Boss.

Boss listened to what the detective had told him, but continued reading through the paperwork on Malcolm Jr. He then turned the page and froze after reading something that caused a small smile to spread across his lips. "Ain't this some shit!"

"What's that?" Wright asked, staring at Boss and seeing the smile on his face.

"It's just a small world!" Boss said as he closed the folder. "I'ma have a little something extra for this in your payment this Friday."

Boss climbed out of the SUV and walked back around to the sidewalk where Trigger and the others all stood waiting for him. Boss then stopped in front of his team.

"What did your rat have to say?" Trigger asked.

"He just brought me something I asked for," Boss answered, holding up the folder. "I'ma have some new shit for the team tomorrow, so I'ma want everybody on point and ready early tomorrow."

"What's up now, nigga?" Eazy asked Boss.

"I need to handle something real quick, but put Butter, Joker, and Black Widow in the three lieutenant spots, and have Butter and Joker at the meeting tomorrow."

Boss dapped up with the team, and then he and Trigger walked off and headed to Trigger's truck. Boss got in the passenger side while Trigger got behind the wheel.

"Big bruh, what's the deal?" Trigger asked as he started up the truck and began driving off.

"You remember shorty I told you about who I met at the gas station in the Porsche SUV?" Boss reminded him. "This is that folder I told you about that had that nigga Malcolm's records inside it. But look who else's name is in it!"

Trigger looked over the papers Boss held out for him, and he read out loud the name that Boss pointed to: "Destiny Moore!"

"That's the same bitch that I met at the gas station!" Boss told Trigger. "Read this right here!"

Trigger looked back at the papers and read out what Boss was pointing at: "Step-sister Destiny Moore and step-mother Patricia Warren!"

"This bitch thinks she's slick, baby bruh!" Boss said with a smirk. "She knew who the fuck I was, and now she's trying to play the setup game."

"So what we gonna do?" Trigger asked, hoping Boss was about to let him have some more fun.

"Relax, baby bruh!" Boss told Trigger, knowing what his boy wanted.

He pulled out his phone and pulled up Destiny's number and hit send. He then looked over at Trigger and said, "I've got a plan for shorty."

"Oh, now you decide to call me, Boss," Destiny answered the call after two rings with a little attitude.

"My fault, shorty," Boss told her in a soft voice that turned into a lowered voice. "Let me make it up to you. Can I see you tonight?"

To Be Continued . . .

*Text Good2Go at 31996 to receive new release updates via text message*

# BOOKS BY GOOD2GO AUTHORS

# GOOD 2 GO FILMS PRESENTS

**WRONG PLACE WRONG TIME WEB SERIES**

**NOW AVAILABLE ON
GOOD2GOFILMS.COM & YOUTUBE
SUBSCRIBE TO THE CHANNEL**

**THE HAND I WAS DEALT WEB SERIES
NOW AVAILABLE ON YOUTUBE!**

**THE HAND I WAS DEALT SEASON TWO
NOW AVAILABLE ON YOUTUBE!**

**THE HACKMAN
NOW AVAILABLE ON YOUTUBE!**

To order books, please fill out the order form below:

To order films please go to **www.good2gofilms.com**

Name:_____

Address:_____

City: _____ State: _____ Zip Code: _____

Phone:_____

Email:_____

Method of Payment:     Check      VISA      MASTERCARD

Credit Card#:_____

Name as it appears on card: _____

Signature: _____

| Item Name | Price | Qty | Amount |
|---|---|---|---|
| 48 Hours to Die – Silk White | $14.99 | | |
| A Hustler's Dream - Ernest Morris | $14.99 | | |
| A Hustler's Dream 2 - Ernest Morris | $14.99 | | |
| Bloody Mayhem Down South | $14.99 | | |
| Business Is Business – Silk White | $14.99 | | |
| Business Is Business 2 – Silk White | $14.99 | | |
| Business Is Business 3 – Silk White | $14.99 | | |
| Childhood Sweethearts – Jacob Spears | $14.99 | | |
| Childhood Sweethearts 2 – Jacob Spears | $14.99 | | |
| Childhood Sweethearts 3 - Jacob Spears | $14.99 | | |
| Childhood Sweethearts 4 - Jacob Spears | $14.99 | | |
| Connected To The Plug – Dwan Marquis Williams | $14.99 | | |
| Flipping Numbers – Ernest Morris | $14.99 | | |
| Flipping Numbers 2 – Ernest Morris | $14.99 | | |
| He Loves Me, He Loves You Not - Mychea | $14.99 | | |
| He Loves Me, He Loves You Not 2 - Mychea | $14.99 | | |
| He Loves Me, He Loves You Not 3 - Mychea | $14.99 | | |
| He Loves Me, He Loves You Not 4 – Mychea | $14.99 | | |
| He Loves Me, He Loves You Not 5 – Mychea | $14.99 | | |
| Lord of My Land – Jay Morrison | $14.99 | | |
| Lost and Turned Out – Ernest Morris | $14.99 | | |
| Married To Da Streets – Silk White | $14.99 | | |
| M.E.R.C. - Make Every Rep Count Health and Fitness | $14.99 | | |
| My Besties – Asia Hill | $14.99 | | |
| My Besties 2 – Asia Hill | $14.99 | | |
| My Besties 3 – Asia Hill | $14.99 | | |
| My Besties 4 – Asia Hill | $14.99 | | |
| My Boyfriend's Wife - Mychea | $14.99 | | |
| My Boyfriend's Wife 2 – Mychea | $14.99 | | |
| Naughty Housewives – Ernest Morris | $14.99 | | |
| Naughty Housewives 2 – Ernest Morris | $14.99 | | |
| Naughty Housewives 3 – Ernest Morris | $14.99 | | |

| | | | |
|---|---|---|---|
| Naughty Housewives 4 – Ernest Morris | $14.99 | | |
| Never Be The Same – Silk White | $14.99 | | |
| Stranded – Silk White | $14.99 | | |
| Slumped – Jason Brent | $14.99 | | |
| Supreme & Justice – Ernest Morris | $14.99 | | |
| Tears of a Hustler - Silk White | $14.99 | | |
| Tears of a Hustler 2 - Silk White | $14.99 | | |
| Tears of a Hustler 3 - Silk White | $14.99 | | |
| Tears of a Hustler 4- Silk White | $14.99 | | |
| Tears of a Hustler 5 – Silk White | $14.99 | | |
| Tears of a Hustler 6 – Silk White | $14.99 | | |
| The Panty Ripper - Reality Way | $14.99 | | |
| The Panty Ripper 3 – Reality Way | $14.99 | | |
| The Solution – Jay Morrison | $14.99 | | |
| The Teflon Queen – Silk White | $14.99 | | |
| The Teflon Queen 2 – Silk White | $14.99 | | |
| The Teflon Queen 3 – Silk White | $14.99 | | |
| The Teflon Queen 4 – Silk White | $14.99 | | |
| The Teflon Queen 5 – Silk White | $14.99 | | |
| The Teflon Queen 6 - Silk White | $14.99 | | |
| The Vacation – Silk White | $14.99 | | |
| Tied To A Boss - J.L. Rose | $14.99 | | |
| Tied To A Boss 2 - J.L. Rose | $14.99 | | |
| Tied To A Boss 3 - J.L. Rose | $14.99 | | |
| Tied To A Boss 4 - J.L. Rose | $14.99 | | |
| Time Is Money - Silk White | $14.99 | | |
| Two Mask One Heart – Jacob Spears and Trayvon Jackson | $14.99 | | |
| Two Mask One Heart 2 – Jacob Spears and Trayvon Jackson | $14.99 | | |
| Two Mask One Heart 3 – Jacob Spears and Trayvon Jackson | $14.99 | | |
| Wrong Place Wrong Time | $14.99 | | |
| Young Goonz – Reality Way | $14.99 | | |
| | | | |
| | | | |
| Subtotal: | | | |
| Tax: | | | |
| Shipping (Free) U.S. Media Mail: | | | |
| Total: | | | |

**Make Checks Payable To:**
**Good2Go Publishing**
**7311 W Glass Lane,**
**Laveen, AZ 85339**